Asher's Secret

SARAH LAMB

Contents

Dedication

For Lynne. I hope that we are writing together for a very long time.

Chapter 1

1878 Spring Falls, Kansas

Asher Steele crossed his arms as he leaned against the side of the sheriff's office. His office. It was a beautiful spring afternoon. Couples young and old walked arm in arm or hand in hand strolling through town. They didn't know how lucky they were. Carefree. In love. Light and happiness around them.

All things he'd never have. Couldn't ever dare hope to have. The thought made him frown, like it always did. He knew that was the price, though.

The only thing he had to offer was the chance at heartbreak. Asher didn't even let himself wonder what it would be like to have a sweetheart of his own. It was too dangerous.

He was too dangerous.

The bakery across the street beckoned, tempting him with a distraction. Some men might want the saloon, but not him. Never stepped in it, except to break up a fight. If he was offered a drink there, he'd refuse with a polite "no thanks." No need to risk it, not with his past.

The bakery, however, was nourishing to the body and was a welcoming place, especially to a bachelor. Taken in moderation, a few treats never did a body harm and not having to piece together every meal was something he appreciated.

Asher looked over his shoulder to where his deputy, Jeff, sat reading the newspaper at his desk.

"I'm going to get some coffee and a fritter if they've got any left," Asher called over. "What do you want?" He didn't have to say where he was going, Jeff could near read his mind at times.

"The same," Jeff said. "It's been too quiet today." The deputy stood up then, and yawned and stretched. "I don't like it, and want to stay alert. If something's brewing, I don't want to doze off and miss it."

With a quick nod, Asher strode across the street. Jeff was right. There was something in the air that just didn't feel quite right. It was too calm. The kind that made a man feel tired and lazy. The only way to not fall prey to the trouble that could cause was to stay alert. One of the bakery's heavy apple fritters was just the ticket. While delicious, they also sat like a lump in the gut and made you feel restless.

Just what the doctor ordered.

The smells of the bakery hit him smack in the face and set his mouth to watering. Asher chose quickly, before he walked out with a half dozen pastries, and accepted the brown paper bag and his mug and Jeff's. They visited so frequently, each man kept a mug at his desk specifically for the bakery to fill.

Asher made his way back to his office, handed Jeff his mug and fritter, and took his back to his spot in front of the building. Resuming his leaning spot, he alternated bites of the fried fritter with slow sips of the dark brew and took in the town.

While he'd grown up not too far away, Spring Falls was his home now. Given that name because of the freshwater spring that was on the outskirts of town, many people had flocked to the area, himself included.

Though the town had only been established for about ten years, it had near doubled in size over the last two or three. Overnight, it seemed, buildings had popped up faster than you could say howdy.

They just about had it all in this town, a barber, general goods store, dressmaker, shoemaker, blacksmith, doctor, and dentist. There was a livery close to his sheriff's office, the bakery, a hotel with a restaurant, a small diner, and a feed store that was right next to the saloon. Just on the edge of town was the church building on Sunday, but the school building the rest of the days. It also made for a good meeting building.

While the town might be a good size, it luckily wasn't prone to too much trouble and he got by just fine with the one deputy. If he needed more men, there were a few who were deputized in emergencies, and none hesitated to answer his call.

But that never was really needed. It was quiet, usually. And the fact it was quiet today should have made him feel better, but it didn't.

As he stuffed the last bite in, a shout came from the end of the street and he spotted three young boys running as fast as they could, the blacksmith chasing after them.

"I better not see you hanging around my forge again!" the smith roared.

Asher pushed up and quick as a flash had two of the boys by their collars, noting the third in the arms of his deputy. "What's all this?" he asked, as the blacksmith panted up to them.

"These ruffians were throwing rocks at my forge," the smith growled.

"That so?" Asher looked down at the squirming boys in his grasp. "Should I lock them up?"

"There's room," Jeff said.

The blacksmith scowled as he took a moment to think. "I guess not," he finally said. "But you boys better not get near my place again."

With scared faces, the three nodded, and ran off as soon as they were released. Asher turned to the blacksmith. "No one hurt?" he asked. "Any idea why they were doing such a thing?"

"Being young and dumb," the smith sighed. "But I can't let it slide, or who knows what they will do next time."

"I agree," Asher said. He tipped his hat up. "That's the trouble with some youth. Some adults too. Got away with pranks and mischief as a child that turned into something more serious as an adult."

"Don't help none that one of those boys is spoiled rotten," Jeff agreed. "Makes it harder when the parents don't take no mind. Spare the rod, spoil the child."

With a grunt of agreement and a wave, the blacksmith turned, heading back, while Jeff joined Asher looking over the town. "Guess that was the trouble we felt brewing," he remarked. "Though, I still wonder if there's something else. It was over too quick."

Asher rubbed at an ear. "I agree." He let his gaze travel again over the people of the town as they walked leisurely, not even the least interrupted by the shenanigans a moment before.

"Becky's glad you were able to come for dinner last night," Jeff said, moving closer.

"I appreciate you having me," Asher said. It was true. Jeff's wife, Becky, was a fine cook. It was nice to have a few meals here and there to break up the monotony of his own cooking, or that at the boarding house, and a weekly meal there was always looked forward to.

"Said it before, say it again," Jeff remarked. "You need to get a wife too. Becky's the best thing that's ever happened to me."

"Not interested," Asher said and crossed his arms. "I tell you that every time you bring it up." He frowned. "Not planning to settle down. Got my reasons."

"When the right one comes along, you will," his friend chuckled, and patted him on the shoulder. He walked back inside and Asher heard the crinkle of the newspaper once more.

"Not likely," Asher muttered. That was one thing he was sure of. He couldn't ever get married, no matter that he'd like to. It was the only way to keep the woman, whoever she would have been, safe from a man like him.

Chapter 2

The stagecoach jerked to a stop and Isabelle Bowman waited impatiently for her turn to climb out. Her legs felt like jelly and she needed to use the necessary in a most urgent way, but she'd put up with all of that, or more, if she could just keep traveling.

Unfortunately, she was almost out of money, and didn't have enough to go even one stop farther. She hoped that she'd be able to find some work as soon as possible so she could be on her way again.

The urge to look over her shoulder was strong, but she didn't dare. Doing so would give it away that she was a woman on the run. With one hand raised to block out the sun, she took her bag that was handed down from the driver and asked, "Is there a boarding house nearby?"

"Yes'm," the man answered. "That large white house down the way."

Isabelle turned to where he pointed. Good. It wasn't far. It also looked over the town, so she could watch who came and who went, if she desired. And she did. "Thank you," she answered, and started walking in the direction of the lodging. Perhaps they wouldn't be too expensive.

The town seemed a good size. Large enough to offer employment and to blend in with the population. There appeared to be a wonderful variety of stores, and perhaps one would hire her. She stepped briskly from the street onto a small walkway leading to the boarding house. "Please be an affordable vacancy," she whispered.

Her knuckles were raised to knock when the door opened suddenly, and two women stood there, a young one with her bag being unceremoniously pushed out, the other an older but spry looking woman, yelling, "I don't tolerate thievery. Out you go, girl. Quick, before I call the sheriff. I can't believe you!"

The first ran down the walkway without hesitation, and Isabelle found herself under scrutiny from the second woman. The look was so menacing, she took a half step back. "Can I help you?" the woman finally asked.

"Yes, I came to inquire about a room," Isabelle said. If only there had been another choice, she'd have taken it. She wasn't sure this woman was someone she wanted to live with—not even for just a few days.

"I've some openings," the woman said. "I'm Sarah Donovan. I'm sorry you had to see that. I'd hired that girl to help me keep the rooms cleaned, and caught her stealing twice."

"That's terrible," Isabelle said. Then an idea came to mind. "Does that mean that you could use some help, as well?"

"It all depends," Mrs. Donovan said. "I don't cotton to thieves. Are you one?"

"No, ma'am," Isabelle said. "My name is Isabelle Bowman, and I'm traveling to California. However, I miscalculated my expenses, and I need to work before continuing on."

Mrs. Donovan squinted at her. "You a mail-order bride? Usually it's the man who pays for all that."

"No, I'm not," Isabelle said. The idea wasn't unappealing though. Why had she not thought of that sooner? A name change, a husband...it was the perfect plan to escape and stay in hiding.

Except for one thing, she reminded herself. Wasn't she running away from a forced marriage? In fact, she was so put off by the idea, she didn't intend to ever marry. Especially a stranger. Admittedly, she could do worse than be a mail-order bride. Most anyone was preferable to what her brother had arranged. If she hadn't left when she did, she might not still be alive.

"Miss Bowman?"

Her head snapped up. "My apologies. I'm a bit tired from the stage."

"Understandable," Mrs. Donovan answered. "I've never appreciated being crammed in those things when I visit my friend Dorothy Meeks in Cottonwood Falls. And it's just a short ride. I can't imagine days in it."

She stepped into the house and motioned for Isabelle to walk in. "If you follow me, I'll show you to your room. You can have it and two meals daily in exchange for helping clean the rooms, plus a dollar and a quarter a week. Is that satisfactory?"

It was less money than she'd have liked, but more than fair, considering her meals and room were included. Honestly, it was unlikely she could do any better. "Thank you," Isabelle said. "I am appreciative."

She followed the other woman through the house and down a long hallway. They stopped in front of a door, and Mrs. Donovan unlocked it. Isabelle looked beyond. The room was small and simple, with just a single bed, a few hooks on the wall, a washbasin and stand, and a chest, but it had a nice window, looked clean, and was most welcome.

Her body ached from the stagecoach jolting, and the lack of room while being squeezed in with so many others. The bed looked inviting, and she was eager to stretch out on it, and not feel cramped for the first time in days. Even the floor would have felt luxurious compared to the coach.

"You can start tomorrow morning," Mrs. Donovan said. "Your duties are fairly simple. I send out the laundry, so you just need to change the bedsheets and towels once a week, dust the rooms, make sure the windows are wiped down, and also tend to the parlor and front foyer daily. You'll rotate so that you do one of the guest rooms a day, plus the parlor and foyer."

"That's all?" Isabelle asked. That sounded quite easy, really. The pay seemed more than reasonable now.

"Yes. Takes about three or four hours a day," Mrs. Donovan said. "Maybe less. The rest of the day is yours. I've a woman who helps me cook and clean the kitchen."

"It sounds perfect." Isabelle said. Perhaps she'd be able to take in a little sewing or a few hours at a shop to help her income grow faster.

"We've a quiet house," Mrs. Donovan continued. "The sheriff lives here. Takes some of his meals here, too. Since sometimes his hours are odd, I do let him do a cold meal or two in his room."

The sheriff? Isabelle felt her stomach clench in worry. What if her brother had shared what she looked like? He had threatened to tell everyone she was deranged. Was she being looked for? Was this sheriff going to send her back to Pennsylvania where she'd worked so hard to get away from? She swallowed, her throat too tight to answer, and nodded. The smile she plastered on her face she was sure looked sickly, but perhaps the other woman wouldn't notice.

After telling her where she could wash her dress, Mrs. Donovan left and closed the door behind her. Isabelle sat on her bed and looked around. Her good idea of stopping in this town and asking for work suddenly felt very worrying. Of all the places to find lodging and a job, she had to do it right where the sheriff lived.

Her mistakes were piling up.

Chapter 3

"Quiet day, Sheriff?" Mrs. Donovan asked, heaping his bowl with chicken and dumplings. She dropped a large piece of cornbread on the top.

"Fair enough," he said. He wasn't in the mood for talking, not that he usually was, but tonight even less. A woman sat at the table he didn't recognize. He didn't want to say something that could be construed as gossip, and have this stranger go around repeating it as gospel.

The boarding house owner saw him flick his eyes the woman's way, and said, "This is Isabelle Bowman. She's traveling through, but staying on until she has enough money to keep going. I've hired her to clean the rooms, so you'll likely see her a time or two outside of meals."

He nodded. "Hello," he greeted Miss Bowman.

Her eyes darted to his face, the badge on his chest, and then away. "Hello."

Without meaning to, his eyes narrowed slightly. That was a woman with a secret, if ever he'd seen one. However, as long as she hadn't brought trouble to his town, he wasn't going to worry about it.

But what if *she* was the trouble? The thought flicked through his mind as he spooned up his dinner. Sometimes the pretty ones were troublemakers, and Miss Bowman was nothing if not pretty.

Wide blue eyes, dark brown hair, creamy skin, slim fingers, a soft voice, and a shy demeanor. He was willing to bet a steak dinner at the hotel that she was anything but meek. Yes, better to keep his eye on this one.

Asher continued to eat, listening as the others spoke. He did that often, and didn't like to get involved unless it was in his line of work. Of course, at times a man could also learn some useful information that way.

Miss Bowman was quiet too, answering a question here and there, vaguely as she could he didn't miss, but also keeping her head low. She seemed focused on her meal, nothing wrong with that, but almost seemed too quiet. Too intent on the plate in front of her,

Mrs. Donovan brought out an apple pie, and he'd just taken his first bite when there was a knock on the door. A moment later, Jeff came in. "Sorry to bother you folks," he said by way of apology, as his eyes fixed on Asher. "Got ourselves a missing woman."

There was a clank as Miss Bowman's fork fell. Red faced, she picked it up, while Asher studied her from the corner of his eye. Was that her story? She'd run away? Was missing?

"Is she in danger?" Asher asked, then shoveled in his pie, ready to head back to work the moment the last bite was done.

"No, she's the danger," Jeff said. "From the Smith place next town over. Had been working for them for a while. She up and left, took Mrs. Smith's diamond necklace she likes to flash around."

Asher groaned and shook his head. "How many times has that woman been told not to show that thing around?"

"Not enough to stick, evidently," Jeff said, hitching his thumbs into his waistband. "We're riding out in a few directions to see if we can find the woman. He looked at a scrap of paper and read, "Blonde hair, brown eyes, birthmark on the side of her neck."

"Alright." Asher stood, and put the last bite in. After chewing, he addressed one of the men at the table, "Ben, you able to ride along?"

Ben was the barber. He dined here instead of cooking for himself, though he lived above his shop.

"Of course," he said. "Let's get going."

Asher picked up his hat from the nearby side table, waved it at Mrs. Donovan, and left. As he was closing the door behind him, it didn't escape his notice that Miss Bowman was several shades paler than she'd been at the start of the meal.

He doubted she had anything to do with the theft, but something had evidently shaken her. Her behavior at dinner made him curious. He made a note to check and see if there were any other missing women in the area.

A woman had the right to run if she was in danger, and if she was in danger in his town, it was his duty to assist her. However, if she was there for some other reason like to cause problems, he'd run her out faster than she could pack her bag. He didn't allow for trouble in his town.

Asher had made that clear from the moment he'd accepted the badge. He might have a curse on him and a black past, but he'd be hung if he let anything from that, or any no-gooding from other folks, hurt this town. Not under his watch.

Chapter 4

Tucked in bed, the soft blue blanket pulled high to her chin, Isabelle shivered. She couldn't seem to get warm. Ever since she'd learned the handsome man at the dinner table was the sheriff, she'd felt panicked.

Then, to make matters worse, when the deputy had come in about a missing woman, her hands had started shaking so badly she'd dropped her fork and everyone had stared at her. Worst of all, the sheriff had fixed her with a look so searing she was sure he'd seen right through her soul. And all the half-truths and unanswered questions she'd been giving that evening.

At dinner, being the new face, she'd been asked about herself. All those usual questions that most people wouldn't mind answering. "Where are you from?" and "Do you have any family?" and the usual "Where are you going?" and while not wanting to offend anyone or seem unfriendly, she also didn't want to share her secrets. The more she told about herself, the easier it would be to find her.

Isabelle gave a little snort of amusement. Imagine if she'd just flat out answered. "Oh, I'm running away from my brother, who is forcing me into marriage so that he can both be rid of me, and make his friend wealthy when they share my inheritance. I'm heading to California because that's about as far away as I think I can get. There, I plan to hide and spend the rest of my days hoping he doesn't come after me. If he finds me, he'll either drag me back or else murder me on the spot in a fit of rage."

Yes, of course. A simple explanation. They'd understand that. No judgment. Right?

She turned over and tried to get comfortable on the lumpy mattress. The pillow was as thin as a pancake, but it was still much better than the stagecoach. Even more importantly, it wasn't costing her anything. With a sigh, she folded the pillow in half and tried to get comfortable.

It was no use. She couldn't sleep, even if she was finally warming up and her trembling had stopped. Since that first day nearly two weeks ago when her brother had told her she'd be marrying—that afternoon—Isabelle had been a ball of nervous energy. A small doze here and there had somehow sustained her, but she just couldn't relax enough to get the proper kind of rest she knew was needed.

This small place, Spring Falls, the sign had proclaimed, seemed nice enough. But it didn't matter. She didn't feel safe anywhere at all. Not while she was being hunted. She needed to find a second job so that she could get out of here as soon as possible.

Her thoughts flitted back to the sheriff. He and his men were out looking for that woman who had stolen a diamond necklace. Once they found it, and the person responsible, she wondered what they'd do. It seemed there were a lot of thieves in the area, between that one and the girl whose job she'd taken.

Luckily, she had almost nothing at all to lose should a thief set their eye on her. Three dresses, her boots, her hairbrush, and not much else. It didn't make her much of a target. And made for faster travel.

How much money would it take for her to get a little further before stopping again? She'd need to enquire. Staying here wasn't a good idea, yet Isabelle had no other option. She was getting her room and meals and a little pay. All was needed. Still, she didn't like to be in one place long. It made her nervous. So did the sheriff, and she planned to keep her distance from him.

Isabelle got up and walked to the window, pulling the blanket tight around her. She looked through her window to the town beyond. It was late, and no one was out, allowing her to take her time observing without anyone thinking she was staring at them.

Spring Falls, though only lit by the moon's glow, seemed peaceful. That must mean there was very little in this town that upset folks, other than thieves, she thought. Back in her own home, Westover, it was always bustling. Frantic. No one looked twice at you. That also meant that no one looked out for their neighbor.

She couldn't count the number of times there had been a crime and no one had witnessed it. It wasn't because the crime was done in the dark or away from eyes. No, it was because everyone had always thought someone else would report it, or else they were too unconcerned, or perhaps too concerned, to let the authorities know or call for help.

In the West, it seemed that wasn't the case. Everyone knew everyone and seemed to look out for each other. That would both make it hard to hide, and also a blessing once she settled down somewhere and made friends. Was it a genuine thing, this seeming to care for their neighbors? This wasn't the first time she'd wondered at the friendliness and open curiosity that everyone she'd met had.

A shadowy figure stopped on the opposite side of the street just then. Isabelle drew back, her chest suddenly tight with fear, hoping she hadn't been seen. In the darkness, it was impossible to tell if the person was looking her way or not, but she didn't want to take a chance it was her brother.

Though unlikely it was him and she'd had a small head start, the fact remained that each day she lingered in any one place put her more at risk. Isabelle slowly backed up, got into bed, and focused her eyes on the ceiling. Her whispered voice quivered, and the uncontrollable shivering started again.

"Please, God. Help me out of this mess."

Chapter 5

Asher flipped through the stack of notices that had arrived on the morning mail wagon. Most of the time, nothing there concerned him. Today, however, he was searching through the list of missing people, criminals, and warnings for other towns, curious as to if he'd find out anything about the boarding house's newest occupant.

As Mrs. Donovan hadn't seemed bothered about the woman who had arrived, he supposed he should trust her instincts. After all, she was a woman who had been taking in strays of all kinds for decades. Still. That wasn't the kind of man he was, nor the kind of sheriff. He took his job seriously, and that included making sure he always trusted his instincts. After all, that's why he was so good at his job—he never doubted himself.

Something about the way that woman—Miss Bowman—had reacted when Jeff had walked in and announced there was a missing woman set his hackles up. He wasn't sure what her story was, and he was hoping to learn it. The town needed to be protected. He wasn't about to let a single soul in his territory down. They depended on him, like a babe its mother, and he was going to protect the townsfolk, no matter the cost.

Asher drummed his fingers on his desk as he reflected, looking up for a moment to check the town through the open door. It was warm today, but a nice breeze came in, carrying with it the smell of the bakery. His stomach growled, and he debated stopping over, but only after he'd gotten through the papers piled in front of him.

A woman walked past and he watched her stop to talk to another woman. She was tall with dark hair, reminding him of Miss Bowman. It wasn't her, though, and he didn't know why he would automatically think about her.

"I've no reason to distrust her," he muttered. "Just something doesn't sit right." He smacked the desk with his hand, letting out a growl. With a heavy sigh, he continued reading each notice before him.

When he came to the final paper in the stack, he shook his head. Nothing. Nothing important, nothing to be concerned about, nothing about Miss Bowman. Why had he expected there to be?

He leaned over to push the papers into his desk drawer. That's where they stayed each time he got them, for about a week, until the stack grew so big, it got taken into a small room and put in a box. Once a month, the box got replaced with another, and then another, until a year, sometimes two, had passed, and he threw away the contents of the first box.

Jeff had laughed at his strange filing system, asking why they needed to keep those old notes, but more than once, they'd come in handy and he was sure it would happen again. His deputy would warm to that, Asher was sure. Notes such as these were valuable. Even if he didn't need them often, it was good to know that they were nearby.

In fact, he wondered if he should head into the backroom and look through the previous week and month's notices. Perhaps there'd be something there about Miss Bowman. And if not, that should set his mind at ease, right? He needed to do that, to clear his mind so he'd stop fretting.

As Asher straightened to stand, something caught his eye. A piece of paper had slipped from the pile and was face down a few steps away. He stood and retrieved it, then his eyebrows shot up.

"I knew it," he hissed. "I knew it."

Folding the paper in half and tucking it into his shirt pocket, he strode to the front of the building where he waited impatiently for his deputy to arrive. It was mid-morning rounds and the two men alternated who went. If all was well in town, Jeff would be back any moment.

If it wasn't, Asher would be hearing about it pretty soon.

Asher strained his ears. Nothing sounded wrong. The town didn't feel like something was happening, either. Beyond this issue with Miss Bowman, that is. Tapping his foot as he leaned against the side of the office, Asher nodded hello to the people calling their good mornings. Finally, he spotted Jeff, who had stopped to talk to someone. As soon as the deputy continued on, Asher waved impatiently, and Jeff walked faster to meet him.

"What's wrong?" Jeff asked. He jerked his thumb backward. "I was just letting the folks know we got Mrs. Smith's necklace back. I think just about everyone knew of it, and kept asking." He chucked then, "The more I tell, now, the fewer I'll have to do later, as fast as gossip spreads in this town."

That was the truth. News hardly left a mouth and traveled to an ear before it was coming out the next pair of lips and flying to a new listener. Often with a little bit of embellishment added on. That was part of why Asher kept his past to himself.

Asher reached into his pocket and produced the note. He lowered his voice. "The new woman in town at the boarding house."

"The one who was acting funny when I went in there?" Jeff's eyes were focused, hard even. He took his job as seriously as Asher did.

"That's right. I think this might be her," Asher said, offering the paper. "Look."

Jeff read the note to himself, and then aloud. "Missing woman. Danger to herself and others. Twenty-one years of age, medium height, dark hair. Traveling by stage, won't have luggage. May call herself Isabelle Bowman."

Jeff looked up then. "My word. That's the woman, alright. What's she done?"

"That, I don't know," Asher answered, his voice tight. "I intend to find out, though. I want you to stay here. Watch things."

"You don't mean to confront her, do you?" Jeff asked. "By yourself?"

"I do," Asher answered.

"I don't like that idea," Jeff said with a headshake. "Be careful. Who knows what kind of danger she is."

Asher nodded in agreement. "One thing I don't understand though," he admitted, rubbing his chin. "If she's missing, why is she using her real name? Why isn't she trying to hide?"

"Might not be smart enough," Jeff answered. Then his eyes widened. "I'll be. Look." He nodded toward the left.

There was the very object of their discussion, walking out of the bakery hurriedly. Asher pushed off the building and quickly fell into step alongside her.

"Miss Bowman," he said politely.

"S-Sheriff," the woman stammered, and stopped.

"How are you finding the town?" he asked.

"It's very nice," she answered. He didn't miss the twisting of her fingers around her small handbag. Was there a derringer in there? He eyed the shape of her bag. No, nothing looked bulky. It was quite small.

"Walk with me," Asher said, leaving no room for argument.

Miss Bowman didn't say a word, simply fell into step with him. He could sense her unease. It near spilled from her every pore. If that was because she was scared or anxious, he couldn't tell. Both emotions felt about the same to him. There wasn't a sense of potential harm to him, though, so he projected calm outwardly, even if he didn't feel that way.

Neither spoke until they reached a cluster of benches sitting near a large oak tree at the bank of a creek. He nodded to the bench and she sat on one end. The woman seemed to fold in on herself, shrinking almost, and the trembling of her hands was visible.

Asher sat on the other end and faced her. "Miss Bowman," he said. "My job is to protect this town and everyone who lives in it."

She nodded. "Of course."

He continued, "Last night, the way you were acting at dinner made me think that you were hiding something. I'm going to ask you straight up about it, and hope you tell me the truth." He looked at her sternly, trying very hard to ignore the frightened look in her eyes that made some small part of him want to stop talking and simply pull her into his arms. "Why are you here?"

"I told you," she said, her voice nearly a whisper. "I'm trying to get to California. But I don't have enough money. So, I had to stop and find work so I could continue on."

"That's the only reason?" he asked.

"Yes," she answered.

"You got flustered when you heard about a woman missing," Asher pressed.

"Of course! I was concerned," she replied.

"Could be," Asher agreed. "And also could be you're a liar."

She sucked in a breath, and anger flashed across her beautiful face. The upset seemed to fuel her then, sparking a reaction he didn't expect from the woman who had been near cowering a moment before. "I am not a liar," she said, her back straight and her eyes fixed firmly on his. Her glare challenged him to argue the point.

"Then I think you'd better tell me the truth," Asher told her. "All of it." He reached into his pocket and pulled out the notice. "My deputy has seen this as well. We know the woman in this note is you. So, now I want to know who you really are, why you are in my town, what threat you pose here, and why you've run away."

Chapter 6

Isabelle couldn't seem to pull her eyes off of the note the sheriff had handed her. Her chest felt tight and she closed her eyes for a moment. She was such a fool. Of course, he'd have sent out her description. And known that she'd have used her mother's name.

She took a deep breath. "I have not lied," she repeated. "I have, though, omitted portions of the truth."

"That's about as good as a lie," the sheriff said, and he leaned back against the bench, arms crossed. "Something tells me, though, that you've got a good reason for it, whether or not I like the omission of your facts. I'm offering you the chance, only this one chance, to tell me what it is before I wire that you are here and lock you up."

Isabelle gasped then, and jerked forward, grabbing his hand before she realized she'd done it. "No! Please don't! He'll hurt me!"

"Who will hurt you?" he asked, leaning forward with a frown. "Is that why you ran?"

Her eyes burned with tears then, and to her shame, when Isabelle blinked, they fell, spilling down her cheeks. "My brother," she hiccupped. "And then he'll force me to marry that evil man, before...before..."

She stopped then, the only sound her sobs she tried to muffle through her fist. Then a hand was on hers, pressing a clean handkerchief into it. "Here," the sheriff said, his tone softer.

"Thank you," she whispered, and wiped at her eyes.

"Start from the beginning," the sheriff said. "I've not made up my mind yet what I'm going to do."

"What about your deputy?" she asked anxiously. "Will he have wired already that I am here?"

"Not until I say so," he assured.

She nodded. What to explain first? That was the hard part. Isabelle bit her lip and then pressed them together. What was most important to say? How much information did the sheriff need? There was no sense in holding any of it back, she guessed. Though it was unlikely he'd even help her—no one could—at least perhaps he'd leave her be and let her keep traveling and get herself to safety.

"I hardly know where to start," she said. She shook her head, feeling frustrated. "I'll just start talking. Tell you things in the order they happened?" At his nod, she continued.

"My real name *is* Isabelle. Bowman was my mother's maiden name, and we share the same first name. I was named after her. Now that I think about it, it was very foolish of me to use that name when traveling." She laughed and shook her head. "I suppose I should have given myself a different name. You'll understand though, when I say that my real last name, Shivenhisen, is so unusual, it's easily recognized. Anyway, a month ago, my father passed away. My brother took control of the family finances, and by default, me as well, since I am unmarried," she said.

"What of your mother?" the sheriff asked.

Her voice grew quiet again. "My mother passed away some few years ago. I lived with my father caring for him until his death. My brother returned home from wherever it was he had been living at the news."

"Go on."

"Father had never forced me to marry. He encouraged me to study and learn all that I desired. He told me when the time was right, I'd find the man I wanted to marry." Her hands clenched into fists then. "He'd left me an inheritance. Five thousand dollars. The same as my brother was to receive. However, instead of giving it to me, my brother decided he'd only give it to my husband. A man of his choosing."

"That happens," the sheriff said. "He's likely within his legal right as well, which I'm sure you know. Is that why you ran away? You disagreed with his choice?"

"No," Isabelle said. "I ran away because they were going to murder me on my wedding night." At the shocked look on his face, she couldn't help but give a tight smile. It almost made her laugh that the cool sheriff, who seemed quite unflappable, was taken aback by her comment.

"You see," she explained, "my brother's voice is quite loud. I overheard him talking to his friend, a Mr. Johnson."

"Did you ever see what he looked like?" the sheriff asked.

"No, I did not," she admitted. "At least, not for more than a second and as he was leaving, and only once. I mainly heard his voice."

"Go on. How does this man come into the story?"

"Mr. Johnson is a man who removes problems, legally, he claims. The plan is to marry me, kill me, and they split my inheritance. Evidently, according to Mr. Johnson, it's very simple and he's done it before. It will look like an accident and no one can claim otherwise."

The sheriff shook his head. "Forgive me, miss. I understand that sort of thing can happen, but I have a hard time imagining that any brother would want to do that to his sister. Especially one as pretty as you are."

"I'm not his full sister," Isabelle said. "That is perhaps part, if not all, of the reason and indeed, makes it even easier for him to be rid of me. You see, my mother was his father's second wife, and Joel, that's my brother's name, never got over the fact that his father, our father, had remarried.

"Joel thought it was a betrayal of his father's love for his mother, and resented both me from the time I was born and my mother. That's why I hardly saw him. So, you see, if I am gone, but he has all his father had left as his own inheritance, it's as though I never existed. He gets his revenge upon my mother, and removes me from his thoughts as well."

The sheriff wasn't looking at her, but staring off into the distance. Isabelle sat quietly, waiting for him to speak. After a long silence, he did. "And you are sure this is the truth?"

"I am," Isabelle said. "I swear it to you." She met his eyes.

"What a story." He sighed heavily, letting his eyes take in the town. His words were slow, filled with consideration as he spoke again. "I can honestly say I've never had to deal with something like this. Murders for revenge or money aren't uncommon, but to force a woman to marry, then kill her? Both at once? And a woman?" He shook his head, almost as though he were talking to himself. "What is the world coming to?"

Isabelle didn't answer. How could she? She had no answer. It wasn't for lack of wondering. That was all she'd been doing. Was it possible to truly dislike someone as much as Joel hated her?

The sheriff stood and looked down at her. There was something in his expression she couldn't decipher, but it made her heart quicken. Fear? Apprehension? She was sure it was some of each, but...there was something about his eyes. They seemed to take in all of her at once. Capture her. It was...almost welcome. Wanted.

What was wrong with her? She needed to get herself out of this town, not let herself be taken in by a pair of piercing eyes and the concern shown by a handsome stranger. He was a sheriff, for goodness' sake. And one who might send her back to her brother.

But what if he didn't? What if he could help her? He spoke repeatedly about this being his town...his people to protect. If she stayed here, would he protect her as well? A tiny flicker of hope formed.

"I'm not sure yet what I'm going to do," he said. "The crime you are accusing him of is heinous. While I'm not saying you are lying, I also don't know you or how trustworthy you are." He crossed his arms over his chest again.

Isabelle felt her jaw drop. Then she closed it. "Of course," she said, lowering her head. All thoughts of him being of help to her fled at once. Instead, she felt stung by his words. Abandoned once again.

"I've got to get back to the office," he said. "I'll figure out what I'm going to do by suppertime. We'll speak more soon. Don't leave town. I'll know."

He walked away, leaving her with his soggy handkerchief in her fist, and a terrifying sensation in her stomach.

All of her running might have been for nothing. He didn't believe a word she'd said.

Chapter 7

"Do you believe her?" Jeff asked.

Asher had told him exactly what Miss Bowman said, over a couple of cups of coffee and some oatmeal cookies from the bakery. They were inside of their office, sharing a desk while they talked low. The note was between them, and now and again Asher would look at it and frown.

Jeff's question made him think for a moment before he answered. He was sorely conflicted about what he thought, and that wasn't like him at all. Usually, he made his decision and stuck with it, listening to his gut. For some reason, his instinct seemed to have taken a trip and left him on his own to figure this out.

"I don't know what to think," Asher said finally. There was no need to hide his frustration. Jeff would understand. "I do think she's telling the truth. The story though...what brother would do that? That's the part that keeps coming back to me and I don't understand. I don't think she's making her story up, but I just can't fathom that. Not even my parents would have done something like that, and they sure weren't good people."

"Some men will do a lot for money," Jeff said. He took a deep swallow of his coffee. "Especially if they think they won't get caught. Too bad she used her real name. She's right, wasn't smart of her. No different from Mrs. Smith, waving that blasted diamond necklace of hers around."

Asher nodded, but didn't answer. He kept replaying the conversation he'd had with Isabelle earlier. Though her distress had been genuine, he couldn't get the image of her face out of his mind. Her eyes had been fearful. A person couldn't pretend the way she had been acting. Worse yet, she was breathtaking sitting there, her beautiful eyes wide, her lips trembling. He didn't like the fact that he couldn't stop thinking about that as well. Even when she'd gotten upset, she was attractive. She'd shown spunk, something he liked in a woman.

Not that he was interested in a woman. No. Which was why he needed to stop thinking about that. About her.

"It's not too late, if this is real, for her to become a mail-order bride and change her name for real," Jeff mused. "There's that office opening up in the next town over."

"You are right, and that's not a half bad idea. That all said, I'm not sure that's what she wants," Asher said. "I admit, were I a woman, I'd be hesitant. She might rush from one bad situation into another."

Besides, though he wouldn't admit it, he didn't like that idea. He couldn't imagine Isabelle in someone's arms. Being kissed by them. Asher frowned. Where had that thought come from? He'd only met her the night before. Up until an hour ago, only suspicion had filled him when he looked at her. Where had the jealousy come from?

It must just be because she was now a member—even if temporary—of his town, and it was his duty to keep her safe. That was all.

But still. No. He wasn't even going to suggest she become a mail-order bride. He just needed to figure this out, see her problem safely solved, and get his mind focused back on where it should be—his job. Not on a woman.

Jeff shrugged. "Just thinking," he said, and took another gulp of coffee.

"What we need is to find out if her story is truthful," Asher said. "I'm not sure how we can do that without tipping off her brother or whoever it was who put the notice in."

"Could just ask for more details, on account of us being a stage stop," Jeff suggested. "That was a traveling note. Sent from town to town for quite a ways."

"Expensive, that," Asher mused. "Means they want her back real bad."

Jeff nodded. "Guess they do, if they can't get that five thousand dollars any other way."

Asher drummed his fingers on top of his desk. He could wire for more details. He could also trace the note's origin and also seek out information about Miss Bowman's brother, but something told him if he did, it would only lead the man right here. That wasn't a good idea. He wouldn't do anything that put her or his town at risk. Not if he could help it.

He looked up then, realizing Jeff was staring at him. "I'm sorry. I was thinking. Did you say something?"

"I just asked if you wanted me to try and find out more."

"No, I don't think so," Asher said. "The more I think on it, the more I'm inclined to believe every word is the truth, and there's no reason to do anything more than keep an eye out, and protect her while she's here. Miss Bowman is anxious to leave the town, and while I can't say if that's the best plan for her or not, I'll respect her wishes if that's what she wants. I'll also try to think up a way to keep her protected while I walk back to the boarding house."

"You gonna let Mrs. Donovan know?" Jeff asked.

"I better," Asher said, and stood. "You doing the evening rounds tonight? I'll go ahead and leave now. Catch her before she serves supper."

Jeff nodded. "We'll keep this between us for now, but it's good there are a few men we can call on if trouble comes knocking."

Asher paused by the door and rested his hand on his revolver. "I've got a feeling that the trouble you and I felt rolling in yesterday is right here in town and it's about to get real big, real fast."

Chapter 8

Isabelle finished sweeping the floor of the parlor and hurried to put the broom away. After her unwelcome talk with the sheriff earlier, she'd asked around town for any small jobs that could be done in addition to her duties there at the boarding house. There were none.

When she'd come back and explained her predicament to Mrs. Donovan, the woman had promised to keep an ear out. While slightly reassured, Isabelle was anxious to start traveling again, and get as far away as she could from her brother and the sheriff.

If only he weren't so good looking, she fumed. How could a man that handsome, with hair the color of honey, be so stern?

She guessed it was because of his job. You had to have a strict exterior, accept no nonsense. And yet...he'd surprised her when he'd handed over his handkerchief. Isabelle had scrubbed it clean in some of Mrs. Donovan's laundry soap so that she could return it to him, but when she'd first pressed it to her face to wipe her eyes, his scent had filled her nostrils, almost rendering her unable to think.

Leather and coffee. That's what it had smelled like. She closed her eyes and breathed in. Almost. She could almost smell it again. A shiver ran through her. It was a much nicer smell than her brother had, his being one of heavy liquor and stale cigars.

The front door opened, and she heard heavy footsteps. Even though she knew it wasn't her brother, because she had just recalled him, her heart still quickened for a moment and she forced herself to calm. The faint trickle of Mrs. Donovan and a man talking quietly reached her ears.

Though it wasn't any of her business what they were discussing, she was done sweeping, and wanted to put the broom away so that she could once again try to find another job to do. The sooner she found one, the sooner she'd have the money that she needed in order to leave.

Mrs. Donovan looked up as Isabelle walked through the doorway. Her usually smiling face looked serious. Isabelle saw the man who was standing there, and her stomach sank. It was the sheriff. Was she about to be turned away?

Where would she go? The stage wouldn't depart for several days—not that she could even afford the fare.

Isabelle bit her lip. She had nearly nothing, and not a thing she could sell. Whatever was she going to do? An incredible sense of dismay filled her, though she tried not to let it show, and refused to let her shoulders slump in discouragement or fear.

"Miss Bowman," Mrs. Donovan said. "Come have a word with us in private, please."

"Yes, of course," Isabelle stammered. She set the broom into the corner of the foyer and walked behind Miss Donovan down a hallway. She was keenly aware that the sheriff was right behind her.

The three of them entered Mrs. Donovan's small office. A round table was near a window, with four chairs around it and a lamp in the middle. The maroon curtains were open, overlooking the street—the same view that Isabelle had from her own window.

Like the rest of the house, the floors were a worn, honey-colored wood, with braided rag rugs here and there, including one in front of the small fireplace.

Mrs. Donovan took a seat and motioned to the sheriff and Isabelle. Isabelle slid into a chair, her hands in her lap, and the sheriff sat next to her. His nearness made her feel uncomfortable. Was he that close so he could arrest her? Trying not to draw attention to herself, she looked for any sign of restraints.

"I have heard something disturbing," Mrs. Donovan said, her fingers laced before her, and concern etched on her face. "It appears that you are a woman on the run."

"I am," Isabelle said, her voice even.

She was proud of herself for that because it was all she could do not to tremble. Her eyes darted between the sheriff and Mrs. Donovan. She remembered how the older woman had chased out the girl the day she arrived, and hope the same wouldn't be done to her. She'd much prefer to leave on her own, with her dignity intact.

"However," Isabelle continued, "I promise I'm not trying to bring or cause trouble to anyone. I'm trying to leave it behind me. That's why I'm working so hard to find an additional source of income. That said, I will leave tonight if you request it."

"You can't," the sheriff said. "There's no stage for another week."

"Then I will walk," Isabelle said, pressing her lips together as shame flooded through her body at the words she knew she must say. "I don't have the fare for the stage, anyway."

"That's nonsense," Mrs. Donovan said, waving one hand dismissively. "However, I didn't realize your situation was so dire. The sheriff has told me that you are in danger. I won't send you away to meet it head on."

"I don't understand then," Isabelle said. She spoke slowly, as she tried to puzzle out why she was there, if not to be sent on her way. "Why did you want to talk to me?"

"Because we must keep you safe until the stage does come," Mrs. Donovan said. "If, in fact, leaving is the safest choice for you."

"I'm not sure it is," the sheriff said. He dropped his head into his hands for a moment, then raised it, looking right at her. "Leaving means you'll be on your own."

His concerned eyes met hers, and Isabelle felt a warm sensation in her stomach. No one had shown care for her needs for so long, she felt overwhelmed with gratitude. That's all that feeling was, she told herself. Not any sort of attraction. The sting from his earlier words faded slightly.

"I've been on my own for a while," she answered lightly. "I can manage again."

"Yes, but you were familiar with the area," the sheriff argued. "If you are traveling, you'll have nowhere to go, no idea who you can trust."

"Another sheriff," she replied. And then, so as to look unconcerned, she added, "But I'm sure it's quite unnecessary."

He shook his head then, as did Mrs. Donovan. "Dear, you can trust the sheriff here," she said. "But he is right. Not all men with badges are trustworthy. If you leave, you might be in more danger. Especially if money is involved."

Isabelle looked at her fingers. They were clasped so tightly together that the knuckles had turned white. How was she to answer them? It was getting harder to pretend that the entire course of events didn't upset her. At her very core, she felt betrayed. It was still difficult to understand how her brother could do this. She had known him her whole life.

Eyes closed for a moment, Isabelle took a shaky breath. She knew they were right. But she couldn't stay. It was the worst thing possible to do! That made her a sitting target. At the same time, she couldn't leave. She had no funds. What was she to do? Neither was a good situation to be in. Silently, she thought a prayer and hoped someone was listening.

"We will figure this out," the sheriff said. His fingers drummed on his knee. "I have a plan."

"A plan?" she repeated dryly. "What kind of plan?"

He took a deep breath. "I'll pretend you're going to be my wife."

Chapter 9

The moment he said it, Asher wished he could take it back. At Miss Bowman's shocked expression, he was regretting his words even more.

"No, I don't think so," she answered. Her voice was prim, her tone disapproving.

"It's a good plan," Mrs. Donovan interrupted. "Everyone knows the sheriff is unmarried. A beautiful woman like you traveling alone? Being a mail-order bride is the perfect reason."

"Why can't I be a cousin or something?" Isabelle asked, her gaze a challenging one. "Why does it have to be a woman about to get married?"

"Because I can't stay as close to a cousin as I need to stay in order to protect you," Asher answered.

"And just why do you feel compelled to protect me?" she asked.

Her posture was stiff, her voice tense, but Asher didn't miss the wobble in her voice, or the small quiver of her lip. Mrs. Donovan didn't either. Asher wasn't sure how to answer. He didn't expect this reaction from her. Granted, he didn't know Miss Bowman well, or at all, but that wasn't how he thought a woman would react when he offered his protection.

She was in a dangerous situation, wasn't she? Her life was at risk. He wasn't a harsh man, and wasn't unclean or hideous to look at, so why did she say no? It confused him.

He stopped himself from rubbing a hand over his face, trying to scrub away the frustration he felt over this whole situation. He'd give anything to have had her never arrive in his town, with her confusing story and face he couldn't get out of his mind. But he had to do his duty. His job. What he knew was right. He wanted to yell at her, tell her to be reasonable and just listen. Instead, he took a longer look at her.

He studied her the way he would someone he was questioning. Looking for the telltale things that would give away how she was really feeling.

Then it hit him.

Fear. Reluctance. Because of marriage. He understood her reaction then. Of course. After all, she was fleeing an unwanted marriage. Did she think he was trying to trick her into a real one?

Asher cleared his throat. "It's all pretend," he assured her. "Trust me, I have no intention of getting married. Not ever."

It was Miss Bowman's turn to frown. Her soft lips opened to speak, when Mrs. Donovan put her hand on the other woman's arm and said softly, "Dear, there's not a better idea. At any of the stage stops, no matter how brief, it's possible, no, it's likely, you were seen. To be helpful, your description and your direction will be given to whoever is looking for you. They'll mean no harm by it, only seeking to help the man looking for his sister who needs care."

Asher nodded. "And they'll be searching town to town for you once they find out you were seen."

"Then it's even more important that I leave," Miss Bowman cried, jumping up from her chair.

Asher grabbed her elbow. "It's not safe," he repeated. "You shouldn't even leave the boardinghouse."

Her eyes were wild with fear, and he wasn't sure she even saw him. Her head was turning side to side, and she darted her eyes about like a caged animal looking for an escape.

Mrs. Donovan's eyes met his. "I'll get some tea," she murmured, and left.

The moment the other woman was gone, Asher surprised himself for the second time that day. He pulled

Miss Bowman into his arms and held her tightly. Her stiff body stayed that way for a moment, then she suddenly grew limp as she sagged against him. Carefully, he lowered her into the chair she had sprung up from.

"I'm not asking you to marry me," he said, kneeling in front of her and holding her hands. "I'm also not going to force you to do anything you don't want to. But if you—we—pretend you are here to marry me, and then you leave suddenly, it's much less suspicious when I tell everyone I didn't like you, or you didn't like me, compared to a strange woman visiting our town for a week or two and then leaving."

Her eyes had calmed as she looked at him now. Asher took that as a good sign. She was giving him her full attention. He kept his voice low, soothing. "I know money is a concern. I'll give you what you need."

As she shook her head no, he stopped her. Her soft skin underneath his hands would have been his undoing, had he not been so firm in his resolve.

"Why are you doing this?" Her question was so soft, her eyes so pleading, that Asher felt a strange rhythm in his heart. He cleared his throat. "Because this is my town. And it's my duty to protect everyone in it. That includes you."

She searched his face, but didn't answer as Mrs. Donovan walked back in. The older woman set a tea tray down. "Is everything settled?" she asked.

"I believe so," Asher said. There was a question in his voice though, as he looked at her.

"Yes," Isabelle answered, her voice low.

"Good," Mrs. Donovan said. Then she smiled at them both. "There's just one thing that you need to do now."

Chapter 10

"Asher. Asher. Ash-er." Isabelle made a face at the mirror, and watched her lips. "Aaaashherrr."

No matter how she said it, it felt incredibly strange to say the sheriff's name. It was a good thing this was all just pretend. She couldn't imagine calling him that day in, day out.

Had it really only been a few hours since he'd made the suggestion they pretend to be engaged? Mrs. Donovan had promised to let it slip "accidentally" to the other borders, so that if anyone had thought her strange at dinner the night before, they now understood why. She was a nervous woman meeting her potential groom.

Too worried to be at the table with the others, Isabelle had gratefully taken Mrs. Donovan's offer of dinner in her room. But now, with nothing to occupy her mind, she found herself worrying even more than she had earlier that day. Isabelle wished she had something to read to divert her mind. Better yet, would be physical activity, but what?

The idea of a walk through the small town was appealing, but she wasn't sure it was a good idea. After learning her brother had sent out her description to who knows how many places, she felt nervous. How many others saw it? She was several states away. He must be blanketing every town in every state.

The man would stop at nothing it seemed, to get her and her money. The idea made her feel sick to her stomach. Angry, too. She'd never been anything but kind toward him. In fact, she'd always looked up to him. Tried to be friendly, even when he would be horrible to her, pulling her hair, dropping ink on her dresses, breaking her toys. They were family, and until the moment she realized he was willing to see her killed—and with no remorse—she had hoped one day he would treat her as a sister, not someone he loathed.

Isabelle sat near the window and rested her cheek on her hand as she gazed outside. What a mess she was in. And all because she'd been so foolish as to use her real name, and her mother's last name. What had she been thinking?

There was a knock at her door and Isabelle startled. "Y-yes?" she called, and went over, opening it a crack.

Her eyes widened. The sheriff—Asher, she was supposed to call him Asher—stood there. She opened the door fully, curious as to what he wanted.

"I thought I'd see if you wanted to join me on a stroll," he said.

"Is that wise?" she asked, wondering more than anything else. After all, he knew as well as she did what the situation was.

"I think it's fine," he told her. "Wear your bonnet. We don't have to get close enough to anyone for them to see you. Besides, it's dusk."

"And it won't make you the talk of the town?" she asked, eyebrows raised. "Walking with a woman after dusk?"

He squirmed a little then, and for some reason it made her delighted to see. "Well, Mrs. Donovan already started telling folks we might be getting married, so I don't guess it matters." He met her gaze then, a little too earnestly. "It's for your protection. That's all."

"Of course. I won't argue. A walk would be nice." She got her bonnet and then followed him down the stairs, to the hallway, and then the front door.

"I've got rounds to do tonight," he said. "My deputy was needed for something else. Perhaps you'd join me? And then we can continue our walk if you like."

"What do you do on your rounds?" Isabelle asked, as they stepped to the front of the house, and then onto the walkway.

The evening air was refreshing. Inside of her room it had felt a little stuffy. A strong breeze blew, carrying with it the scent of Mrs. Donovan's flowers. Fragrant roses and lilac filled her nose. Isabelle closed her eyes for a moment, and raised her chin, letting the fresh air caress her senses. It felt wonderful. The sort of thing she was sure she'd never be able to get enough of.

"Well," Asher said, pulling her back into the moment, "I walk past the front of the shops, check the doors and make sure they are locked, peer in through each window, and continue both sides of the street."

"It's almost like window shopping," Isabelle laughed.

"I supposed it is," he grinned.

He slowed, but as two women paused on the opposite side of the street, looked their way and giggled, he cleared his throat and started moving again, grabbing her elbow. Isabelle hid her smile at his obvious embarrassment.

"Do you get much trouble here? For the merchants? I know thievery must be a problem. I know of at least two instances my first night."

As they started walking, Asher gave a small shrug. "Thieving and mischief making are the most of it," he told her. "I don't think it's ever going to matter if a town is small or large. Too many folks out there see something they want, even if it's not theirs, and feel entitled to take it."

"I understand," Isabelle said. "Is that why you became a sheriff? A strong sense of justice?"

The sheriff stopped at the barber's shop, tugged on the door, then moved to the shoemaker, doing the same before he answered. "In part."

"What's the rest?" she asked.

He stopped then, and looked at her. "Honestly, I'd rather not say."

"Why not?" Isabelle asked. Then she demanded, "You've ferreted out my secrets. It's only fair you return the favor."

Asher frowned then, looking away in the distance, then started walking again, this time checking three doors before he answered. When he did, his voice was low.

"It's because I'm cursed. There's bad blood in me, and I'm doing all I can to make amends."

Chapter 11

When Isabelle—it was hard to think of Miss. Bowman by her Christian name—had asked him his reason, it was on the tip of his tongue to simply go along with her suggestion that he was a man bent on delivering justice. It was true, in a way, but there was more. So much more.

But what would she think if she knew? The thought tugged at his mind as he checked the shop doors. She was right, in part. He knew her secrets, and it would be fair if he told her his. The thing was, though, his secret wasn't hurting anyone, and it also didn't have the potential to.

Hers, however…it put her life at risk, and anyone else around her. Her story was two very different things.

Miss Bow—Isabelle's eyes were on him as he checked the next door. He was all too aware he'd not answered. He stopped then. What did it matter? He might as well tell her. Maybe knowing that she wasn't the only one who experienced a difficult past would give her the encouragement that she needed to know her future was of her own making, not that of someone who was deciding for her.

Voice low, so it wouldn't carry even though no one else was around, he finally answered, "It's because I'm cursed, and I'm doing all I can to make amends."

Asher didn't miss her curious look. "Cursed? What do you mean?"

"Let's just leave it at that," he answered gruffly, unwilling to share any more.

"No, we won't," she answered, and put her hands on her hips. Her eyes sparked with the fire he'd seen in them earlier. "If I'm to be engaged, pretend or not, I deserve to know just what you mean by cursed."

The idea of telling her about his past life shook him. No one knew. Not even Jeff. Maybe it was because he felt no one would understand. It could also be he didn't want people thinking that because he'd grown up the child of two people who couldn't care less about the law, that they'd look down on him. Suspect him of dirty dealings.

If he thought about it for a while, he might even reach the conclusion that it was because he didn't want to somehow put his curse on her. Asher wasn't sure, and he opened his mouth to tell her, again, he wasn't planning to tell her anything else.

But what came out, when he met her fiery expression, wasn't what he expected.

"There's bad blood in me. It goes way back. A couple generations at least. I figure if I keep to myself, work hard to do good, and take care not to pass it on, maybe I can break that curse." He started walking again, and had checked another two shops before she'd caught up.

"Wait. What do you mean? I don't understand what you are saying."

Asher hesitated. He didn't really want to explain it further, and shrugged. He started to walk forward when she grabbed his arm. A warmth spread through him with such a surprise that he turned and looked at her, his legs feeling heavy as lead.

Isabelle squeezed his arm gently. "I'd like to understand. Please."

He looked at her hand, and she must have misunderstood because she started to remove it. Before he knew what he was doing, Asher put his hand on top of her own. The smallness of her surprised him. Her hand seemed tiny next to his, even though she was as tall as his shoulder. Each finger and the nail was perfectly formed, and a sudden desire to press his lips to her palm came over him.

Just as quickly, he pushed it away. He knew much better than that.

Taking a deep breath, Asher explained, "You see, my folks weren't good ones." They reached the last door to check on that side of the street and crossed over to check the rest of the shops. "Growing up, my parents only were concerned with two things. How much was left in their bottle, and how they'd get more when it ran out."

"I'm sorry," Isabelle said softly. "So, they neglected you?"

"That's one way of putting it," Asher answered. "Beat me too. Pretty often. When they got drunk, they got angry. Real angry. I was a good target. And more often than not, they were drunk."

Isabelle sucked in a breath and stilled. Asher stepped backward to stand next to her. His voice quiet, he continued, "My grandparents were the same. I was the only child, and when I was growing up I made a decision. I'd break whatever curse this was on our family. I wouldn't drink, I wouldn't treat anyone that way, but instead I'd look out for them."

She nodded then, and her gentle squeeze reminded him that her hand was still on his arm. He liked the feeling of it. It was comforting.

Clearing his throat from the sudden frog in it, he continued, "I figured that way, if I did those things, I could stop whatever cycle my family was in. I'd be the last, and it couldn't continue."

"That makes sense," Isabelle agreed. Then she tilted her head to the side. "But you are leaving something out."

He walked to the next store, and her hand was still on his arm. If she left it there the rest of the night, he wouldn't mind. It would look good too, he told himself, realistic, in their pretend engagement. It wasn't because he found her attractive.

"Part of that means that I'm not going to get married. If I don't get married, then I won't have kids. If I don't have kids, I can't pass this bad blood to them, and keep this going."

"Asher..."

He didn't hear what she said for a moment, too caught up by the sweet way she said his name. He liked the sound of it on her lips. As Isabelle kept talking, he caught more of what she said.

"What you say is very noble. I don't think I'd expect anything less, not from you. In the short time I've been here, I can tell that you care very deeply. But I can also tell you, that you aren't to blame for your parents or grandparents' actions. You also shouldn't be carrying on the burden of change, either."

He shrugged, and continued to walk, checking the doors. "I disagree," he said mildly.

"I've learned the importance of understanding that we can't take responsibility for the actions of others, only ourselves," she said.

"Exactly," Asher said. "That's what I'm saying."

"But—"

The hairs on his neck stood up, and Asher stopped. In a quick motion, he reached for the gun at his belt. Something wasn't right. The door to the bank wasn't shut all the way. A faint sound could be heard from the backroom. Thieves? How many?

"Get behind me," he whispered roughly to Isabelle, as the wind pushed the door open slowly.

Chapter 12

Isabelle's heart felt as though it had leaped up into her throat. The sheriff had his gun in his hand faster than she could blink, and was standing in front of her.

She didn't think anyone had ever put themselves between her and the danger. The tenseness in her body was mixed with an unexpected feeling of relief. She felt, oddly, quite safe with him right there.

There was a scuffling sound in the building and a dark shadow moved. Asher said, his voice commanding and cold, "Hands up. Real slow, and turn around."

She watched as a small man, shorter than her, turned around, his arms raised in the air and a terrified look filled his face. Her heart thumped faster. Who was this man? Was he a hardened criminal? While he didn't look much like one, she knew from Joel, a body could never take first appearances lightly.

"Sheriff! D-d-don't shoot! It's m-m-me," the man stammered.

"What are you doing here?" Asher asked, lowering his gun and putting it in his holster.

Isabelle stood in the shadow, watching silently, unsure of what was happening. The smaller man lowered his arms, only to start pointing. "Late deposit came in. Went to put it in the bank safe."

"Lock the door next time, Jim," Asher said. "Nearly put a bullet through you."

The other man nodded and hurried over. Asher stepped back outside and watched as Jim reached to lock the door. He waved and disappeared into the back room before Asher could return the gesture.

"Who was that?" Isabelle asked.

Asher looked at her, almost as though he'd forgotten she was there. "Jim Morris. Runs the bank. If you ask me, a little too scatterbrained for the job of bank manager. This isn't the first time he's forgotten to lock the door in the evening."

He looked at her then with that expression of concern he'd worn a few times now. "I hope you weren't scared. I know that was unexpected. Are you alright?"

"It takes more than that to alarm me," Isabelle assured. Then she blushed. "But I must tell you, that was the safest

I have felt in a long time. I've never had anyone protect me from anything before."

This time it was him who reached for her. His warm fingers brushed her own, and she slipped her arm through his. "I'll keep you safe," he said, his voice serious.

The words sent a thrill through her. For a moment, just a moment, she wished this wasn't all pretend. That someone like the sheriff did care for her. Would protect her. The thought made her sad then, and tears pricked her eyes. It wasn't fair. None of it. What had she ever done, but be born?

She'd tried so hard to be a good sister. Her father had never shown either of his children favoritism, so why was Joel so desperate to remove her? Was jealousy and her inheritance really the reason? She wasn't sure. However, there were too many questions, and no answers at all. Such as, how long before he found her? And if he did, could she ever escape? Would she live long enough to have the chance at love and happiness, and perhaps to create a family of her own?

She bit her lip. "I'm scared," she admitted. "Of Joel finding me. What might happen when he does. As I'd told you, he frightens me. Ever since I left, I've been looking over my shoulder, peering around corners, and trying not to draw attention to myself."

"It's understandable," Asher said. "I admit, at first I wasn't sure if I believed your story."

"I don't blame you for that," she answered. She let out a small laugh. "It sounds farfetched, even to my own ears, and you don't know me."

"No, not well, anyway. But after a lot of thinking, I've decided that I do believe your story. My instincts have never proven me wrong. That's why my deputy and I have been watching for anyone new to town."

"That's a little hard," Isabelle said, raising her eyebrows. "Not that I don't appreciate it," she added hurriedly. "It's just people seem to come and go every day here."

"They do," Asher agreed. "But we know most of them. So far, no strangers."

"I'm glad," Isabelle said. She stopped and looked around the town. "It's lovely here," she said. "I can see why so many people come to this town."

"A good number stay on," Asher said. "Especially because of the spring."

"The spring?"

"Yes. The one the town is named after," he told her. "Sweetest water you'll ever taste. Even during times of no rain, we manage to still have plenty of water. Somehow, it never runs out."

"How interesting. I'd like to taste that," Isabelle said.

"Let's go soon," Asher said. "Sunday afternoon. We can picnic over there. A lot of folks do, but I know some of the better spots that aren't ever crowded."

"Oh!" Isabelle was taken by surprise. While she was interested in seeing it, she hadn't thought that he'd actually offer to take her. After all, their relationship was one of pretense. When she looked at him, he was waiting, an expectant look on his face.

It made her smile, and a small flutter of excitement formed in her stomach. It was for the outing, not for being with him, she firmly told herself. "I'd love to," she answered. "That sounds wonderful."

"Good, I'll let Mrs. Donovan know of our plans, and ask if she'd make us a basket of food to take. Bakery is closed Sundays."

"I don't want to be any trouble," Isabelle said.

"You won't be," he assured her. He started walking then, and her arm was still in his, Isabelle realized. It had felt so comfortable, she hadn't even realized it.

They walked together back toward the house, and he paused as they stood on the porch. "Well, goodnight," Asher said, looking suddenly uncomfortable.

His unease surprised her. The sheriff had been so calm ever since she'd known him. Earlier, with the possible threat of a break in, he'd not even hesitated before running into the danger, not away from it. So, why was he hesitating now?

He leaned in closer, and Isabelle's heart nearly stopped. Was the sheriff about to kiss her?

Chapter 13

Asher jerked himself backward. What in the world was he about to do? The surprised look on Isabelle's face showed him that she knew he'd considered—heck, almost did—kiss her.

Straightening up quickly, he leaned against a pillar on the porch and hooked his thumbs into his waistband. "Nice evening," he said, even though it sounded completely foolish to his own ears.

"Yes, it is." He glanced up and saw Isabelle's lips twitching. Was she...laughing at him? He scowled then. Before he could say anything more, she said, "Thank you for the walk. I think I'll retire now, but I look forward to our picnic Sunday."

He nodded, keeping his mouth shut so nothing else stupid came out, and watched as she walked inside. When the door shut, he groaned loudly. What was it about her that kept drawing him in? When he was trying so hard to keep himself back.

What was wrong with him? He knew better than to get involved with anyone, or to let anyone get under his skin the way this woman was. So why was it he kept getting closer to her? Inviting her on walks and picnics? That was the wrong sort of thing to be doing. He was supposed to be protecting her, not wooing her.

A sudden surge of frustration filled him, and he struck the pillar with the palm of his hand. He knew what would happen if he ever courted a woman, fell in love, and married. He'd end up just like his pa, and keep the bad blood going. That's why he had to keep his distance. But now, he had offered and agreed to a picnic. He couldn't retract the offer.

Clenching his jaw, Asher strode off to his office. He needed to get away from things for a while.

He walked down the street, his usually alert eyes not even noticing where he was until he stopped right in front of his office, his legs carrying him there out of habit. There was a lantern glowing inside, and he looked in surprise as he walked further into the building, to the backroom, and saw Jeff surrounded by a stack of papers.

"What are you doing here?" he asked.

"Something's bugging me," his deputy said. "So I wanted to look into it. You told me that Joel fellow's last name, didn't you? Shivelston? Shivelten?"

"Shivenhisen," Asher said. Small hairs on the back of his neck rose. "What's come to mind?" He and Jeff shared similar instincts. If his deputy felt concerned, he was too.

Jeff stopped his riffling through the box and looked up with a frown. "'Bout six months ago, there was a string of bank thefts. Remember that?"

Asher nodded slowly. "I do. The fellows never made it here, though."

"No, but they were never caught, either. A witness to the last one gave testimony to what he'd heard, while hiding outside of the bank being robbed."

"I remember," Asher said slowly. "But I don't remember what it was, exactly."

"I don't fully myself, which is why I want to find it. Might be nothing, but might be something." Jeff shook his head. "I was set for bed when it came to me. Something stuck out to me and I wanted to find it to see if I remembered right."

"Then let's find it." Asher looked for a moment, letting his eyes skim the labels, then pointed to a wooden crate. "That one." He grabbed it and set it down on the floor between them. Both he and Jeff reached in and grabbed a handful of papers, reading over the notes that arrived daily.

The only sound in the office was the rustle of papers. They were nearing the end of the box when Jeff grunted. "Here. Listen to this." He cleared his throat. "Witness claims a man by the name of Silverheim or Shiverstein was the leader of the group. He knew this, because they'd gone to school together, but he couldn't remember the man's unusual last name. All he knew was his first name was Joel." He looked up then.

Asher let out a low whistle. "Coincidence, maybe. But sounds a little too much so. Same first name, unusual last name that starts with a S. Anything else?"

"No." Jeff shook his head again. "That's it. Now, what are we going to do with this information?"

That was a good question. Right now, they had nothing but a suspicion. There had been no crime that could be pinned down on Isabelle's half-brother. That made it difficult for them to do more than watch for the man. On the other hand, if there was a way to prove he'd been robbing the banks, he could be locked away for a long time or dealt whatever justice the judge deemed proper, and Isabelle wouldn't have to fear for her life.

"We've no evidence," Asher said slowly, reluctantly. "But keep this notice out. Let's watch and listen. Like you've been doing, suspect anyone new. Even a woman. A man like that, who knows who his accomplices are. He could buy or force anyone.

"If Isabelle's brother is the man who robbed the banks, he's dangerous. That gang kills without hesitation, I heard tell. We all know what happened at Walnut Ridge when they went through last year. Six dead, and three of them women, one with her babe."

"I agree," Jeff said. His voice dropped, and when he next spoke, a chill ran right down Asher's spine. "If it's really him, she's in more danger than we realized. A man like him doesn't just kill. He kills for pleasure and with no remorse."

Chapter 14

Isabelle carried the used bedsheets out to the storage room for the laundress. She hurried back up to the room she'd been cleaning and made sure everything was in order. Her eyes drifted around the room while she did her mental checklist.

Bed made with new sheets. Window wiped. Everything dusted. Rug beat. Floor swept. Clean towel. Was there something else she was supposed to do? She frowned and shook her head. No, that was it.

Grateful that she could take a break now, Isabelle started to leave when something caught her eye. A photograph was peeking out from under a chair in the corner of the room.

"Oh dear. Did I knock this over?" she wondered, and stooped to pick it up. As her fingers reached out, she suddenly froze, and her heart started thudding.

A familiar face stared back at her from the photograph. The person was younger, but there was no doubt in her mind who it was. In fact, she remembered that very day her picture had been taken.

The photograph fell from her fingers and she backed away, as though it were a hot stove she'd touched. What should she do? Should she tell anyone or just leave? The idea came to her to take the photograph, but then whoever it belonged to would know she'd seen it. Perhaps Asher would know what to do. Or Mrs. Donovan.

Worry raced through her mind, and she stumbled out of the room, nearly tripping down the stairs. There was only one thought running through her mind right now. *Seek help.* She burst into the kitchen, nearly running over Mrs. Donovan. The woman looked at her crossly, then her face changed. She must have sensed something wrong.

Isabelle's words came out garbled. She couldn't even understand herself. "Photograph...room...it's me." Her voice was high pitched. She looked around frantically. Only one thought was clear, coherent. She must leave. Must. "I have to go," she turned to run out of the room when Mrs. Donovan grabbed her arm. Halted, Isabelle turned toward her.

"I don't understand what you are telling me. You've got to slow down. Calm yourself. Use more words," the older woman ordered sternly.

Isabelle nodded and gulped in a deep breath. At that moment, Asher walked through the door. She pulled herself away from Mrs. Donovan and threw herself at the sheriff. "I've been found!" she gasped, and then nearly collapsed from the relief of seeing him.

Two arms wrapped around her, then pulled her back slightly, though he still supported her. "Tell me," he ordered.

Mrs. Donovan sat them down at the kitchen table, and with a shaking voice, low as she could, Isabelle explained. "I was cleaning room number six. I'd finished, and was just looking once more to make sure I hadn't forgotten to do something. I don't want to make a mistake and upset someone."

At Mrs. Donovan's approving nod, she continued. "Well, there was a piece of paper underneath the corner chair and I realized it was a photograph. I thought I must have knocked it over when dusting, so I went to pick it up."

She stopped then and took a deep breath. Her fingers were clasped together, but they still shook. Were they going to believe her? Think her hysterical?

"Go on," Mrs. Donovan said, impatiently.

"I leaned over and saw it was me. A photograph of me. From about two years ago."

Asher didn't say anything. He froze, then bolted out of the kitchen, Mrs. Donovan right behind him. She heard them thundering on the stairs, and came to the bottom of the steps, just as they crested the top. Isabelle followed, her skirt in one hand, and watched as Mrs. Donovan gave two sharp knocks on the door, then opened it.

There, still on the floor, was the photograph. Asher held up his hand to stop them, but squatted, Mrs. Donovan right next to him to look at it.

"Yep, that's you alright," he said. "But why?"

"I'll tell you all I know," Mrs. Donovan said, "but not here. That might not be safe." Turning quickly, she left the room, Asher and Isabelle right behind her.

When Asher's arm wrapped around her at the bottom of the stairs, Isabelle greedily took the comfort he offered. She didn't care who saw or that she shouldn't. For the first time since she'd seen the photograph, she felt better. Perhaps, even for the first time since she ran.

"My office," Mrs. Donovan said, and didn't speak again until they were in her office, sitting on the chairs around the table. Well, Isabelle and Asher sat. Mrs. Donovan paced.

"I feel sick," Isabelle whispered. "When is the next stage? I must leave."

"No," Asher said. "The best plan is to pretend you don't know anything." Then he looked at Mrs. Donovan. "And we don't. What can you tell us?"

Mrs. Donovan seemed to shake herself. "That room belongs to a Mr. Wimple. I only saw him once, when I let the room to him. He said he was traveling by horse, but wanted to take the stage and was waiting for the next one."

"He knows I'm here. He must suspect I'll be on it," Isabelle said. She felt calmer, more focused. Now she knew that her worst fear had come true, she could make a plan.

"What's he look like?" Asher asked. "How long has he been here?"

"Three days," Mrs. Donovan said. "Medium height. No beard. Strange colored eyes. Almost...yellow"

"Yellow?" Isabelle asked in a whisper. She seemed unable to speak louder. "Who has yellow eyes?"

"Yes," Mrs. Donovan agreed. "Very unusual. I told him point blank he'd be bathing before he set foot in my rooms. He stunk. But he assured me he would. I've not seen him sense. Doesn't take meals with us, or you'd have seen him," she continued.

"No," Asher said slowly. Isabelle could tell he was turning the facts over in his head. "He hasn't. Which makes me think he took the room, found out when the stage was leaving, and went to let your brother know."

Isabelle straightened her spine. "I won't marry him," she hissed. "I refuse to." Her hand was clenched into a fist and anger coursed through her body. This man might try and take her, but it wouldn't be without a fight.

"I'm so sorry," Mrs. Donovan said. She pressed her hands to her face. "I didn't know."

"Of course you didn't," Asher reassured her. He stood and rested a hand on her shoulder. "And it's obvious he wasn't here long enough but to look around, see Isabelle, and make for her brother."

"Why didn't he just take me right then?" Isabelle asked. "Wouldn't that have been easier?"

"My guess is because he's just looking for you, and likely hoping to do it without a fuss. Getting you unaware, like on the stage and at a stop, forcing you off and on some other mode of transportation."

"So what do we do?" Isabelle asked.

"We've got to pretend we don't know anything at all," Asher said. "And wait for him to make his move."

Isabelle couldn't help it. She stared at him, her jaw hung open in disbelief. "That...that's ridiculous!" she said.

"No, it's not. Let me explain," Asher said.

But she couldn't. She just couldn't put her safety—her life!—in the hands of someone she'd only known for a matter of days.

"It was one thing pretending to know you, to be getting engaged to you, when we thought it might keep me safe," Isabelle said. "But it's a whole other thing to keep this pretense up, along with an added one—of acting like we don't know that man is here. Because he is. And I'm not safe. Not when he knows where I am."

"What do you propose, then?" Asher asked. He crossed his arms and leaned back in the chair.

What *was* she suggesting? Isabelle frowned as her mind suddenly emptied. There had to be a better idea, but what? The next stage wasn't coming for a few days, and now, it seemed unlikely that it would be safe for her to even get on it. So, perhaps an escape in the dark? Take a horse and ride?

But to where? She wasn't familiar with the area. That could lead to even more disaster. And she sure didn't have any money.

Pressing her lips together tightly, Isabelle fought back a glare. "Fine," she relented, throwing her arms in the air. "We keep pretending."

Asher nodded, as though he knew she'd say that. "Good. Don't worry, I promise to keep you safe. I won't let any harm come to you." He walked toward Mrs. Donovan's door then glanced back at her. "Don't forget about tomorrow."

"Tomorrow?"

"Yes. Our picnic." He opened the door and left then, filling the room with the sudden feeling of something missing.

Chapter 15

Asher peered into the large basket Mrs. Donovan had packed. "I appreciate this," he said, his mouth already watering.

"I see you are in your best shirt and pants. Planning to show her the sights or woo her?" Mrs. Donovan asked, her back to him as she rummaged for something on the opposite side of the kitchen.

"W-what?" he sputtered. "Just being friendly. Pretending, remember? Isn't this what people do when they are engaged?"

She didn't answer, just gave him a smile when she turned around. "I think she'd be a fine girl for you. You suit each other."

He stared at her then, not even pretending his shock. "Us? No, like water and oil," he said, shaking his head. "Salt and pepper. Couldn't be more different."

"Yet, though different, each complements the other."

He didn't like her smile. Or that look in her eye. It was meddling. Asher thought about telling her so, but the longer he talked to her, the worse she'd get. He knew that from experience.

Instead, with a grunt, he grabbed the basket and strode to the parlor. Glancing down, he looked at his shirt. Maybe he should change. Was it too nice? But wasn't nice how you were supposed to dress taking a woman somewhere? Real or pretend?

The whole thing was getting confusing. So were the feelings that he was starting to have. Last night, he'd hardly slept. He told himself it was because he was worried about her safety. And he was. There was no doubt about that. But each time his thoughts drifted, and it was happening more than he'd like, it was about Isabelle herself.

Her thick, beautiful hair. Her eyes he could stare into all day. Her laugh, that was music to his soul. There wasn't anything about her he didn't like, didn't want to protect, didn't want to keep for his own and love and cherish for eternity. How was it that he'd been able to look at plenty of women and never feel a thing for them, but with her he felt differently?

That was dangerous. So was this continued line of thinking.

"Asher? Are you ready?"

Isabelle's soft voice broke him from his thoughts, and he realized she was standing in front of him. Clearing his throat, he nodded. "Yes. Sorry. Was lost in thought."

"Has there been a development?" she asked worriedly. "About Joel?"

"No," he assured her. "Just was mentally making sure I had everything we needed for our meal."

She glanced down at his hands and the heavy basket. "From the looks of that, we'll have more than enough."

"I agree. Ready to go? I have a wagon out front."

Isabelle nodded and opened the door for them. Asher set the basket in the back of the wagon, then offered his hand to Isabelle. She climbed up, and he walked around to the other side and jumped in. After a shout to the horses, they jostled down the dirt road.

Another wagon, one with another couple, came from the opposite direction. Both gaped at the sheriff, and set to talking excitedly. Asher gritted his teeth and wished he could sink down. By the time they got back, the whole town would be whispering about him and who he was courting.

But, wasn't that the plan? He reminded himself this was to keep Isabelle safe. The reminder didn't comfort him though. Instead, he felt an odd mixture of embarrassment that he was caught in public with a woman, when he'd vowed never to be, and pleased that he had such a fine one sitting next to him.

"How far away is the spring?" Isabelle asked, raising one hand to shade her eyes.

"About three miles," he told her. "Well, at least the part I want to take you. It's a real pretty place."

"I can't wait to taste the water," Isabelle said. "Mrs. Donovan said it will be the cleanest I've ever had. I wonder if she's right about that."

"She is," Asher said. "Clear as a crystal, and refreshing."

They sat in silence for a few moments, the only sound the wagon wheels humming along the road. When he stole glances at her, Isabelle was looking around at the scenery, as a tree here and there grew to several trees, then a thicker collection of trees. The tall oaks and maples spread their branches, blocking out the sky. Soon, the sun was forced to peek through the canopy of leaves overhead. The temperature was cooler in here, the light dim.

Birds called from boughs, squirrels ran along the side of the road, and a soft breeze caused the leaves to rustle.

"It's beautiful here," Isabelle said. "Very relaxing and peaceful. Really, I had no idea such a thing existed. Quite a difference from the town, with all the buildings and people and very little greenery."

"It is. I like to come out here," he said, slowing the wagon. They came to a stop and he set the brake, then jumped out, coming around to offer his hand again. "Watch your step," he warned, but a half second too late as Isabelle's foot slipped on the narrow step.

Without thinking, his arms wrapped around her waist, and he pulled her close to him. Slowly setting her down, he didn't realize he was still holding her until she looked up at him with a smile. "Thank you for catching me," she said.

Asher jerked his arms back. "Just doing my job," he said, quickly turning and getting the basket and a large blanket from the back of the wagon. "Keeping the citizens safe."

Even to him, the words sounded foolish, and he wondered why he felt that way so often. Why was it his mouth would spout the most ridiculous of things at times, but only when Isabelle was near? He'd never been like that until she arrived and he started to get to know her.

"I'll carry the blanket," she offered, and took it from his arms.

Their fingers brushed, and he tried to ignore that tingle left behind.

"Which way do we go?" Isabelle asked, turning her head from side to side.

Asher pointed. "Over here. If you listen carefully enough, you'll actually hear it."

They walked in the direction he indicated, and Asher was rewarded when Isabelle gasped.

"My goodness! I've never seen anything like this," she exclaimed.

That was the same reaction Asher had the first time he'd seen the spring. It didn't bubble from the water, but came from a rock opening. Because of that, it spilled down, creating a small waterfall and trickled into a large pool. The glistening rocks shone in the sun's rays, while the tinkling sound of the water rushing over the water was a pleasurable sound, almost as though a melody was being played by nature. His ears would never tire of it.

Asher squatted down and reached his hand into the water. "Cool, no matter the time of year," he told her. "Never has run dry, from what I hear."

"A marvel," Isabelle said, holding her skirts tight as she crouched down next to him. She cupped her hand and dipped it into the water. She brought it to her lips, and he watched as she caught a drop with her tongue. "No wonder everyone speaks so highly of this water! It's unlike anything I've had before."

Asher nodded, and stood then, moving a short distance away. He shook out the blanket and opened the picnic basket.

"Let me help," Isabelle said, and hurried over.

Together they set out a jar of pickles, one of strawberry preserves, biscuits, cold ham, a small wedge of cheese, two apples, and several boiled eggs.

"Goodness! A feast," Isabelle said. "She packed enough for more than just us two."

She helped herself and Asher did the same. There was another moment of silence, but Asher didn't mind. The silences were comfortable. He enjoyed that. Isabelle had this feeling about her, like he'd always known her, and he appreciated it. It was a good feeling to be able to just sit in quiet and not feel awkward. It also felt good knowing that he could be himself.

After a few bites, Isabelle set her plate down. She toyed with the edge of her plate and softly asked, "What will happen when it's time for me to leave? Do you think such a thing will even happen? Can I leave safely to continue on my way?"

Asher felt his heart sink. Of course she'd ask about that, even if he didn't want to think about it. He was enjoying himself these last few days, even if it just was pretend. Playing pretend was the closest he'd ever get to a real relationship with a woman, and he'd miss her once she was gone. It was selfish of him though, and he knew it.

"I think that we'll be able to catch the man who took the room at the boarding house and also your brother," he told her honestly, even if he wanted to tell her she had to stay forever. Pretend to be his forever. "Once that's done, what you do next is your decision."

The words, as soon as he said them, didn't sound right. He tried again. "Not that I'm wanting you to leave."

That didn't sound right either. There his mouth went again, spitting out things he wasn't sure he wanted to say.

"So, you'd like me to stay here?"

Isabelle was looking at him intently. He wasn't sure how to answer. If he should answer. As he tried to form the right words in his head, she leaned back, looking disappointed, and said, "Never mind. You don't have to answer."

"It's not that," Asher said. "It's..."

When he stopped talking, she picked up her plate and took a furious bite. Asher looked down at his own plate and did the same. Why couldn't he say what he meant? More importantly, why couldn't his heart do the right thing and stay away from this woman he hardly knew?

Chapter 16

Isabelle chewed in silence, outwardly looking calm, she was sure, but inwardly furious. A hurricane of emotion swept through her, and though she tried to tell herself that was foolish, she couldn't help it.

It wasn't a good idea to get involved with someone. She knew that. But her heart wasn't being logical. It kept feeling drawn to the sheriff—to Asher—and she had hoped, thought she sensed, that he felt the same.

Of course, she was obviously wrong. She couldn't read people well. That's why she was in this mess in the first place. She trusted too much. Always thought everyone was as forthright as she was. That wasn't ever the case, but still, no matter how often it happened, she couldn't ever learn that lesson. *Don't trust others.*

Just another foolish mistake I've made, she thought, angry at herself. I can't expect others to be how I want them to be. How I hope them to be.

Isabelle peeked under her lashes at Asher, who looked decidedly miserable. She wondered why. When he'd told her his story, she'd felt sorry for him. She still did. She wasn't angry with him. It was this whole mess of the circumstances. Hers, his, it didn't matter. All of them were difficult.

How terrible it must be, to think that you were responsible for the burden of ensuring your bloodline died out, to prevent—real or imagined—something that had plagued your family for generations.

She wondered why it was that he thought such a thing. Surely he could see he bore no responsibility. He hadn't even been alive at the birth of either his grandparents or parents, nor, likely, at the start of their drinking and poor decision making. Where the blame came from, she wasn't sure, unless it was simply the strong feeling of justice he had running through him, that desire to do right and to protect others.

That led to her next thought, and it made her fume even more. He'd said it more than once; she lived in his town and it was his job to protect her.

His job.

Was that all she was? There were times that Isabelle felt she was more than that. But then he always said something that made her doubt. Hesitate. Feel hurt. Get angry.

"I'm sorry."

Isabelle looked up at the unexpected words. "What?" He'd distracted her, and the anger she'd been holding on to slipped away. It was hard to be upset whenever she looked into his face and met his caring eyes.

"I'm sorry. I'm not good with words. And I told you, I can't let myself get involved with anyone. The destruction my bloodline creates must end with me." Asher's voice cracked. "No matter what I might want."

"It doesn't have to be that way," Isabelle told him softly. "You can make your own choice, choose to make good decisions. Help others, look after them, and still have things like love and a family of your own."

He shook his head. "I am scared to," he admitted. "I don't know if I can, without making a terrible mistake."

Isabelle didn't know what possessed her, but she reached over and squeezed his hand. "I'll help," she promised. "In any way I can."

They were quiet again, and something unspoken seemed to fill the air, dancing about and making her wish it would just happen, whatever *it* was.

Asher cleared his throat. "I expect I can't eat another bite," he said. "How about a short walk before we go back?

It gets darker here in the wood, and it's easy to get lost. I suspect we have about an hour before that happens."

"That would be lovely," she answered, and helped him pack the picnic up. They both concentrated on putting the items away, deliberately keeping their hands far apart. It was almost a dance. A choreographed instance. And for some reason, it hurt, even as her hands kept their distance of her own accord.

Asher carried the basket back to the wagon and offered his arm. Isabelle gladly took it, though she had been surprised he'd offered it after what he'd just said.

"The path ahead is mostly well walked," he explained, "but there are a good number of roots. Don't be surprised if your toe hits one and sends you forward. That's why I'd best hold your arm."

Was that all it was? She swallowed back her disappointment. "I appreciate the warning," Isabelle said.

She felt secure holding on to him, and they walked slowly through the woods. Fallen branches grew bumpy, ribbon like fungus in oranges and cream colors, a shy rabbit peered out at them through a shrub, and a bird with blue markings she was too far away to see well hopped from branch to branch above them.

"Do you come here often?" Isabelle asked.

"Maybe once a month," Asher replied. "Not too often. Don't have anyone to do things with like this."

"Are you lonely?" she asked, not ashamed of the intimate question. It didn't seem to bother him, either.

"I'm not sure. Jeff invites me to dinner at least once a week. Sometimes I go, but I get a little lonely feeling seeing him and his wife. Work keeps me busy. There's almost always someone who needs help. Because of that, I talk to a lot of people. Meet a lot of new folks."

He studied her for a moment. "What about you? Growing up with a brother like Joel must have been hard."

She laughed. "I knew nothing else, so I couldn't say. I enjoy keeping to myself, or staying occupied with books. Those are all the company I have ever wanted." She stopped then and looked down. "Until now."

He didn't answer, but there was a light pressure on her fingers. A heavy silence overcame them. Even the forest's sounds—birds, leaves shuffling beneath their feet, twigs snapping—seemed to stop. Isabelle risked a glance at him, and he wore that unhappy expression again.

"We'd best be heading back," Asher said, his tone laced with regret. "I've got rounds, and then an early morning. There's a mail coach coming through in the morning. Often, it has the payroll, so I'm there to see nothing goes wrong."

"That makes sense," she agreed. She knew how seriously he took his job. He was an absolute blessing to the town and its folks. She'd never known a lawman to be so caring of all the citizens of his town. It was as if each were his own.

They walked in silence back to the wagon, where once again Asher helped her into the seat before climbing in himself. They sat closer, perhaps closer than necessary, and the short drive back only made her heart ache worse. To be this close, to know it could never be more because he was scared of any sort of relationship that may hurt her.

There was no way to convince him otherwise, that she knew. Isabelle looked forward to Joel being caught, hopefully soon, and enough money to continue her travels. Spring Falls would have nothing for her but heartache if she stayed. Heartache from the man she was falling for but couldn't have.

Chapter 17

Four days had passed quietly. The man in room six hadn't returned, though Mrs. Donovan checked daily. In the evenings, Isabelle and Asher went on walks and shared stories about their past. Asher told himself to stop, but he couldn't. Each day, he grew more in love with her.

Though he and Jeff had kept a close eye out as well, there was no more news about Isabelle's brother. Asher wondered if he could relax, but didn't dare let himself. That's when things happened; they always did.

"Been a bank robbery," Jeff greeted him that morning, holding the stack of daily notices. "Twelve miles away at Hark Hammer."

"Anyone hurt?" Asher asked, looking quickly through the notes.

"No, luckily. They didn't catch them. Don't have a direction they were going."

"What is this world coming to?" Asher asked.

"No good," Jeff answered. "That's what."

Asher grunted. He dropped the notices on his desk. "I'm heading to the bakery. Get you the usual?"

"Yes, indeed," Jeff said. He patted his stomach. "Get me two. I skipped breakfast."

Nodding, Asher walked across the street. After accepting the brown bag and the mugs of steaming coffee, he stepped into the street. A man in a suit was walking past. Nothing unusual, except for the fact almost no one in town wore suits. He hurried across and whistled low. Jeff came almost immediately through the office door, took his mug, and watched with him.

The two leaned against the building, as though nothing were amiss, but their sharp eyes missed nothing. About six paces behind, another man, also a stranger in a suit, walked, holding a newspaper under his arm.

But their town's paper came out tomorrow. Not today. Could be a coincidence, but might not be.

"Look there," Jeff said quietly, pointing with his mug. "Yonder near the blacksmith."

A covered wagon was sitting, and two men were talking to the blacksmith, who was nodding and looking at something.

"Get closer," Asher ordered, and Jeff nodded, ambling down the street.

A few moments later, the deputy returned. "Broken part. Smith says he'll get it fixed shortly."

"Something isn't right," Asher said. "Four men, all strangers, two in suits? I'd bet a blackberry pie that they know each other, and they aren't here just to pass through."

"I'd take that bet if you weren't the one making the pie, but I'd lose," Jeff said. He leaned in close. "Took a look in the back of the wagon. There's a lot of rope. Like for tying up a person."

Asher took a breath. "Can't jump to conclusions," he muttered, as much to his deputy as to himself.

Just then, Mrs. Donovan came running toward him. She was waving at him, and he straightened. There was a look of anxiousness on her face. "What's happened?" he asked.

"It's him. Mr. Wimple. He's back. He's brought a friend."

Jeff reached out and steadied Mrs. Donovan as she came to a stop. "What's he wearing?" he asked.

"A suit," she said, out of breath. "And his friend, he signed the guest register. His initials are J.S."

Asher stepped closer. A feeling of absolute wrongness filled him, and he fought back an irrational anger that formed. "And you left Isabelle alone?"

Chapter 18

Isabelle yawned. She'd hardly slept for the last few nights. Oddly enough, it wasn't because of her worry over Joel and whoever else it might be after her. It was because of the sheriff.

Each time she closed her eyes she saw his face. It was a terrible feeling knowing that she had a connection with him, and that he felt it as well, but it could never be. For her, though, she knew that perhaps eventually she could find someone else. He never would. Feeling his terrible longing and heartache and despair for an entire life was something that made her feel sad for him. If only things could be different, but one thing she knew was that Asher wasn't likely to change his mind.

He was a man of conviction. Driven, one might even say, to think only of his cause. There was nothing at all that would make him change his mind. He'd sworn it, and she had no reason to think he'd ever think differently, not as determined of an individual as he was.

Isabelle fluffed the pillows on the bed of room three and picked up the dirty sheets. She carefully carried them down the stairs and through the doorway of the kitchen.

"Miss?"

She paused. The load of laundry was so tall she couldn't see around it, but she turned just the same, trying to angle herself to see something. She couldn't. Oh well. She'd tried. "Yes?" she asked.

"I wondered if I might get another towel," the man asked.

"Oh, of course," she answered. The voice wasn't one she knew, but she also wasn't very familiar with the guests there, as she only saw them at some breakfasts or dinners. "If you'll just follow me, there are some in the laundry area," she explained, and turned back around.

"Let me get that door," the man offered, and she heard his footsteps go before her.

"Thank you," she said, grateful because she couldn't really see where she was going.

In the laundry room, Isabelle dropped the laundry on the floor. She'd need to sort it into a large bin once she handed over the towel. The laundress wanted it arranged just so. As she was bent over, she spotted the shiny shoes of the guest. *What an odd choice for a place like this. I wonder if he's some sort of salesman?*

Isabelle reached for a towel, and it was in her hand just as the laundry room door closed, the lock clicking into place. She looked at it, frightened, and then glanced to the other door, the one that led outside.

A man stood in front of it, a gun in his hand and a cruel smile on his face. Isabelle couldn't see who it was. There was hardly any light and his hat was pulled low, but she didn't have to make a guess. She knew.

It was Joel.

A lump formed in her throat and she had to force the words out. "Leave me alone."

He laughed. It was a hard laugh. Full of evil that ran up and down her spine and made Isabelle shiver. "Now, Belle," he said, the nickname their father had given her mockingly on his lips, "I can't do that. You know that. You ran away. That was a very bad thing to do. You've left me, and your fiancée, quite brokenhearted. We had to come get you."

There was nowhere to move. Her back was against the cabinet, and there was a man in front of each door. Isabelle looked around in a panic. Was there a weapon? Anything she could defend herself with? There was the broom, but not much else. Perhaps if she played along, she'd have a better chance of survival.

"Now, why'd you run, Belle? Hmm?" Joel stepped closer, the gun in his hand not wavering.

Outside. She had to get outside. Someone would see her then. *Surely. God, help me please,* Isabelle prayed.

"I overheard you," she said then. Her fingers inched toward the broom. "I don't want to die. You can have my money. All of it. The entire inheritance. Just leave me alone."

Joel shook his head then. "Doesn't work that way," he said. "Can't get the money until we've got a marriage certificate. So you see, I'm in a bit of a situation."

She wet her lips, and shuffled closer to the broom. "Why, Joel? What did I ever do to you? Why do you hate me so much that you want to do this? You don't have to do it. Fake a marriage certificate. Or, or, I'll marry, but then let me go. You'll never hear from me again."

There was a movement to her side, and she looked as the other man stepped closer. "Doesn't work like that, sweetheart." He glanced at Joel. "She's headed for that broom."

With a snarl, Joel kicked it away from her. "You just always have to be so clever, don't you? The smart one. I'm smart too," he growled. "I've gotten away with more than you could ever imagine. You'll just be a distant memory in my mind. I'll enjoy everything I deserve."

"What's wrong with you?" Isabelle cried. "Why did you become so evil?"

He didn't answer. Isabelle knew she might never know why he did the things he did. She just hoped she'd make it away somehow.

"Now what?" Joel asked. His eyes were focused on her, but the question was obviously directed toward the other man.

"Now, we get in the wagon and head to another town to get married. We'll throw her off a cliff or something. Wreck the wagon. You got the alcohol? We'll force her to drink it, and claim she was driving and we couldn't save her. One whiff, they'll understand why." He smirked, "Pour it all over her if you want. I've got two jugs. We could even set it on fire. That's always fun to do."

Joel nodded. "Okay. Let's go. You drive." He reached into his pocket and pulled out a length of rope.

Isabelle tried to bolt then, even though she knew that the door to the house was locked, she still flung herself at it, beating on it and screaming. Maybe Mrs. Donovan or one of the boarders would hear her.

Her hands ached, but she pummeled it as hard as she could until Mr. Johnson grabbed her and shoved a dirty rag in her mouth and tied her wrists behind her. Giving her a shove forward, he snarled, "Go."

She had no choice. When the door opened, Isabelle's heart sank to see that instead of the road, and people passing by, her view was blocked by a large wagon. She was shoved into it, and Joel climbed in the back, his gun still trained on her.

The wagon started, and Isabelle bounced around, unable to steady herself without her hands. Joel's attention seemed to wander as he peered through the back of the wagon. She eyed his gun. If only she could get her hands free.

Her nightmare had come true, and Isabelle knew one thing for sure. He wasn't going to let her live, and she wasn't going to go down without a fight.

Chapter 19

Asher had never run so fast in his life. Jeff was right behind him, and he didn't have to turn around to know that his deputy had his gun out, and would likely veer off to the blacksmith, the barber, and the general store looking for backup.

How had it happened? They'd all be watching so closely. He was angry at himself, but worse, several times he'd promised to protect her. It was possible he'd let her down. Was she calling out for his help even now?

As he raced toward the boarding house, he tried to reassure himself that all was well. That Isabelle was fine. Just because the man had returned didn't mean that she was hurt or taken. She was a clever woman. Resourceful. Careful of her surroundings. She'd made it this far, she could last a little longer.

And he was just letting himself worry for nothing. Isabelle would likely be sitting back at the boarding house, reading or sewing, maybe dusting the parlor.

A covered wagon raced down the street, narrowly missing him. Asher flung himself away from it just barely, then returned to his frantic pace. Coming up to the boarding house, he threw the door open. "Isabelle!" he shouted, and raced up the stairs. He didn't care if he startled anyone or sounded like a fool. "Isabelle! Isabelle!"

Mrs. Donovan had followed him, though at a slower pace and had run to check the room Isabelle was staying in. "Her belongings are still here," she called to him as she went into the kitchen.

Asher thundered down the stairs. "I'll check around back, see if Jeff's seen anything," he said, just as there was a scream.

Spinning quickly, he headed to the kitchen. Mrs. Donovan was standing, pointing at something. He moved closer to see. "What is it?" he asked.

"This door was locked, from the inside," she explained. "You know I always keep the key in this side of the lock, but it wasn't there. I got the extra key and unlocked it. When I opened the door, I saw the laundry here, in a heap." She pointed again, urgently at the pile.

"Okay?" Asher said, confused.

"The laundry goes into the barrel in the corner after it's been sorted," Mrs. Donovan said. "Isabelle knows that."

At first, Asher thought she was upset that Isabelle had done the task poorly. Then he realized what she was saying. "There's a towel on the ground too," he said. "Still partially folded."

"He must have followed her in here, under pretense of needing something," Mrs. Donovan said, bringing her hands to her face. "Poor girl didn't know what he looked like. And if he caught her unaware, with her arms filled with sheets, likely she also didn't get a proper look."

Asher strode across the small room. "This door is unlocked," he said, and opened it wide. He looked out and in each direction of the road. "I don't see anyone. She can't have gone far, not if she was being taken against her will. If she were on her own, I think someone would have seen her. If I know Jeff, he's looking through the town."

As if he'd summoned him, Jeff appeared, and shook his head. "No one's seen her."

"What about the men in suits?" Asher asked.

"No, not seen them either," Jeff said. "However, I did find someone—two someones—you might want to talk to. Just locked them in the jail for safekeeping."

"What? Who?" Asher said as he hurried back to the office.

"You know the men with the wagon earlier that we didn't recognize? Turns out that wasn't their wagon."

"Go on," Asher demanded.

"They were paid to take it to the smith for repairs. They were just about to leave town on their horses and head back home when I caught them."

"If that wasn't their wagon..." Asher turned and ran back to the boarding horse.

"What is it?" Jeff hollered, chasing after him.

"A wagon near ran me over," he said. "It was the same one we saw at the blacksmith earlier. I didn't think much about it," he said as he came to a stop. Asher knelt down, and sure enough, wagon tracks were up against the rear door of the boarding house, the very one he'd gone out of moments before, and Isabelle must have been forced out of.

"She was inside it," he said angrily, and slapped his palm against his thigh in frustration. "She was inside the wagon, and I didn't know it."

Jeff hesitated, looking between the tracks and Asher. "Did you hear anyone call out? You're sure she was taken against her will? Was in the wagon?"

"I feel it," Asher said solemnly. He glanced up and saw Mrs. Donovan looking at him. Her eyes were watery. "Don't worry," he said, trying to sound confident. "I'll get her back."

"But how?" she asked. "They've had a long head start."

"We'll track them," Asher said. He turned to Jeff. "Round up a posse. Quiet men only. Make sure everyone is armed. I'll get my horse and yours. Meet me at the jail. I'm going to question those men, then we'll go."

Jeff nodded, and turned, quick to gather the men they needed. Asher jogged to the jail and opened the door, stopping before two men.

The men had been sitting on the floor, talking quietly. When they saw him, they jumped up. "Sheriff! Honest, didn't do nothing," one stammered.

"We got paid ten dollars each to take the wagon to get fixed. Easy money." The other spoke, truth written all over his face.

"By who?" Asher questioned, crossing his arms.

"Couple men in suits," the first man answered. "Talked funny. Not like proper folks."

Proper folks to these two likely meant someone local. Talking funny likely was someone from out of town. Probably out of state. Asher nodded. "I believe you, but I've a few more questions. You get a name of those men? They've kidnapped a woman."

The first man shook his head, but the second squinted and rubbed at his forehead. "Shiveman. Shinman. No, none of that's right. I know it started with a shhh sound."

"Made me think of shivering," the first man volunteered.

"Got a first name for me?" Asher asked. He didn't want to suggest Isabelle's half-brother's name, and plant an idea in their mind if it wasn't right. At their head shakes, he turned to leave.

"Got a letter, a set of letters of his name," the first man offered.

Asher turned back.

"I don't know my letters put together like," the man explained, "but I recognize some of them. Especially the ones in my name."

"What did you see?" Asher was trying to be patient. He knew Jeff was working on getting the posse together, but he also knew each moment counted. And a moment more was all he was giving to these two men, who didn't seem to be of much help at all.

"There was a fancy travel bag inside the wagon," the first man said. "Had two letters engraved on it."

"Well, what were they?" He was impatient, he knew it, but Isabelle was in danger. The only thing keeping her alive was the fact she wasn't married yet, but how long before a reverend could be found?

"There was a J and an S," the first man said.

That was good enough for him. Asher ran out of the jail, hollering for the boy standing nearby to see the prisoners had dinner, but stayed put.

J.S. Joel Shivenhisen. It couldn't be anything but.

He hurried to the stable, where both his and the deputy's horses were already saddled. Jeff was coming around the corner, and hurried to mount, riding out of the stable. "Got two men with us," he said, as they started the direction the wagon had gone.

Asher nodded. "Let's see how quick we can find them," he said. "Wide spread."

Jeff nodded, and gave the order as Asher galloped out of town, plumes of dust rising behind his horse. The men would ride about twenty feet apart. Enough to still see each other, but wide enough to see something another might miss. Like a wagon.

He leaned low over his horse as they raced. By his estimate, the wagon had a half hour lead on them. A few miles, maybe. But his horse was fast, and Asher was determined. He just hoped that Isabelle knew he wasn't going to leave her.

Hold on, Isabelle. I'll find you.

Chapter 20

The wagon's lurching eased as the horses slowed. There was a shout from the man in the front, and Joel moved around her to stick his head through the wagon cover. "What did you say?"

"Horses need water. And the wheel feels wrong again. We better look at it before it breaks."

Joel muttered to himself for a moment. "Fine. Let's stop."

The wagon slowed further. Isabelle shifted uncomfortably. The ropes dug into her wrists and she ached all over. It felt like they'd been in the wagon for over an hour. She was hot, and hairs clung to the dampness on her forehead, while her mouth felt bone dry. Water sounded more than good.

"Joel," she whispered, her throat too parched to do more than that. "Please, can I have some water?"

He paused, half in and half out of the wagon as they came to a stop. "I guess," he said. "We aren't stopping long, though." He stood and waited, smirking as she struggled to walk to the wagon flap. It was going to be nearly impossible to get down with her arms behind her back, but Joel shook his head. "Nope. Not untying you."

She didn't want to beg. Didn't want to ask for anything from Joel, but she was so thirsty. "Please," she whispered.

The other man came up then, and wordlessly grabbed her from the wagon, setting her down on the ground heavily. He walked away, and Isabelle blinked in surprise, then stumbled toward the creek they'd stopped beside. She didn't know why he'd done that, helped her, but she wasn't going to waste time to ask why. She wouldn't put it past Joel to change his mind about her getting a drink.

The water looked clear, and a small waterfall had formed. The horses drank deeply, and she went upstream from them a few feet. Neither Joel nor the other man tried to stop her, which was surprising, but where would she go? And she sure wouldn't get far, not tied up like this.

Isabelle leaned over, trying to balance herself without falling face forward into the water. She drank slowly, her mouth making small slurping sounds, to her embarrassment, as she hovered over the water. She wanted to buy as much time as possible for Asher to catch up.

Something told her that he was looking for her. There was no way that he would leave her behind.

But then her heart sank. He probably didn't even know she was missing yet. And when he did find out, how would he find her? For all he knew, she'd run away. Or headed east or west...or whatever. Truth be told, she wasn't sure which way they'd traveled. She just knew it wasn't anywhere near Spring Falls.

Yet, why did she feel so sure he'd look for her? There was no guarantee he would. She could be quite wrong. In fact, even if he did, he might go in the wrong direction. The only one she could depend on right now was herself. But it was difficult to discern what she could do with her hands tied.

She leaned back and wriggled herself into a standing position. Joel and the other man were over by the wagon. They seemed to be in a heated discussion. Isabelle took the opportunity to glance around. There was nothing to aid in an escape. Not even the natural cover of a forest. They were on an exposed prairie, which complicated things. There wasn't anywhere to hide.

Her heart beat faster as an idea formed. Wait! No cover at all. That was a good thing! Perhaps someone would see them. Could she stall?

"Isabelle. Get over here." Joel motioned to her angrily. When she froze, and didn't move, he pulled out his gun and growled, "Don't make me use this. Come on."

As slowly as she dared, Isabelle returned to him. Joel shoved her up into the wagon, and took his place again in the back, near the flap. The wagon started, the horses moving at a quick pace. Once again, Isabelle had no idea where they were headed. So much for stalling. If only there was a way to draw attention to the wagon, to perhaps get a rescue.

Joel was peering through the back opening. He seemed distracted. Anxious. This was unlike him. Usually, he was cool and calm. Maybe this meant that his plan was falling apart.

As they rode, Joel never taking his eyes off the back, Isabelle knew she'd have to do something. There was no guarantee anyone would save her. She'd have to figure out a way on her own. There were not many options, but perhaps she could at least appeal to her brother's humanity—if he still had a shred if it left.

"Joel," she asked. "I'm not going anywhere. I can't go anywhere. Can you please untie my hands?"

"No."

He didn't even look back at her. Isabelle gritted her teeth. It would do no good to argue with him. She let her eyes roam around the wagon. A small flap had formed from the cover loosening on the side nearest her. It let in a nice breeze, and a view from the side. Curious as to what would happen, she positioned herself, an inch at a time, so as not to draw attention to her actions, and with great difficulty tugged on the ties of the wagon cover. It released more, the wind catching and helping pull it the gap wider.

Isabelle could see more, and an idea came to her mind. What if she could loosen both sides? Would the wagon's speed rip off the cover? If it did, it would not only expose them, but, if Joel didn't stop, leave the cover as a sign they were there. If he did stop, then it would take time to put the wagon cover back on, delaying their progress.

Isabelle bit her lip as she shot a worried glance at Joel. He wasn't paying a bit of attention to her, and this was the best idea she had. Surely he wouldn't suspect her of doing anything, not with her hands tied behind her. Perhaps it wasn't the best of ideas, but it was something, and she sure didn't have much else she could do.

Patiently and painstakingly, her wrists aching, her hands barely able to move, Isabelle got to work. She just hoped if she could make this happen, she'd figure out the next thing to do. Joel wasn't a patient man. If he didn't get rid of her before the sun went down, it would be tomorrow for sure, as soon as they arrived at a town with someone who could marry her and the driver.

Lord, help me, she begged, as she felt the wagon cover give a little more.

Chapter 21

"Something's ahead," Asher shouted, and pointed. In the distance, about a mile ahead, a trail of dust rose up. Something was also flapping in the wind, but he was too far away to make it out. He urged his horse and rode faster. From the corner of his eye, he saw the others drawing closer.

"Come on, girl," he said to the horse, pressing his knees into her side. The horse responded, but he knew she couldn't go much faster. She was getting tired. They'd been riding for nearly two hours.

"Just a little more," he coaxed.

On the horizon, he could see it better now. A covered wagon. The cover was loose and suddenly broke away. A figure stood and reached for it, grabbing frantically, but missed.

Asher held his breath as he strained to look. There were three figures. One driving the wagon, two in the rear. A man and...Isabelle! He'd found her! His heart leaped with excitement and he pressed on, his complete focus on rescuing her.

The wagon ahead slowed. Asher wasn't sure if they were stopping for the cover or some other reason, then he saw it leaning funnily to the side. The repaired part from earlier must have given out at the same time the cover flew away. This was his chance.

He pressed on, drawing closer, and reached for his gun, just in case there was trouble. He was near enough now that he could see Isabelle clearly, and it was obvious she saw him. She was sitting up, her face looking anxious. Her body was in a strange position, and it took a moment for him to realize she had her arms behind her back.

In the wagon there was a flurry of activity, and Asher pushed his horse, but she couldn't go faster. The posse was drawing closer, but they might not reach her in time. The men had unhitched the horses from the wagon, and Isabelle was thrown over the back of one, like she was a sack, right in front of one of the men he could only assume was Joel.

That lapse in time helped Asher to close the distance. "Let her go," Asher demanded, anger lacing his tone. He was a horse length behind them.

The man with Isabelle laughed. "Not likely," he said. He pressed a gun to Isabelle's body. "I advise you to call your men off, or she's going to get it."

Asher narrowed his eyes, taking a moment to read the man. Then he nodded once, and Jeff and the others dropped back. He kept up though, keeping his own weapon trained on the man. "They're gone. Let's talk. What do you want? Joel, isn't it?"

He was hoping by using the man's name, he'd relax. Feel calm. Friendly. Sometimes it worked. Other times it didn't. When everyone had their weapons out, it wasn't usually going to end well.

"None of your business," Joel replied. "Stand down, Sheriff. Let us go, and I'll let her live."

"He won't," Isabelle gasped.

Joel growled and shoved his gun deeper into her. "Shut up," he said. And then, the expression on his face turned to one of delight. "Wait a moment. You feel something for him, don't you?" The gun pivoted and turned to Asher. "You want to see her suffer? Keep following us."

"I'll see you suffer," Asher growled. "I'm not going anywhere."

"Asher," Isabelle said, "he'll kill me anyway, but he doesn't have to hurt us both."

Her tone nearly tore him in half. He didn't care about himself. Let himself get shot, he was aware of the risk, but he wanted to protect her. How could she, even in this moment, be thinking about him? She was his to protect, not the other way around.

The thought came, and sent a jolt through him. She was...his? He wasn't thinking about her as someone in his town. He was thinking about her because he knew, more than anything else in the world, he had to save her. His life would be nothing without Isabelle in it.

"I'll make you a bargain," Asher called calmly.

"Don't think so," Joel answered. He kicked his horse, tried to go faster, but the horse wasn't having it.

Asher ignored him. "You want her married, right? So you can have her money?"

Joel glanced at him, but didn't speak. Asher took that as a good sign, though. The man was listening. Meanwhile, the posse was getting further behind. He had to act soon.

"I'll marry her," Asher said, "and you get her money. Then we'll both be happy. You go on your way and never return."

He didn't miss Isabelle's look of surprise, nor the blush that colored both her cheeks.

"Not good enough," Joel said. "I'm not interested. What I want, you can't give me."

"And what's that?" Asher asked. From his side vision, he could see Jeff. His deputy was trying to come from the far side, flanking the other man. He had to keep Joel's focus on him.

"I want her to suffer," Joel hissed. "The same way I did, every time I looked at her."

"You've a lot of darkness in your heart, if you want your own blood to suffer," Asher said, with a slow shake of his head.

"Then I guess we don't have a deal," Joel laughed.

There was the cocking sound of a gun and then a shot.

Chapter 22

When Asher had come into view, her heart surged. Isabelle hadn't dared hope, but he'd come. He'd really found her.

From her position, flung over the horse, her head kept bouncing along the saddle, her cheek striking it if she turned one way, her chin knocking her teeth if she did the other. Dust filled her eyes, making them tear. All of that was secondary to the fear she felt in her body.

The cold metal of Joel's gun never wavered, and she knew he was ready to shoot her. It was hard to hear what he and Asher were saying over the hooves of the horses and her position, with her head so low.

Asher rode closer. He was easier to hear now. His familiar voice comforted her, and she thought, at least if I am about to die, it will be with the sound of him nearby, not alone and hurt and terrified.

"You want her married, right? So you can have her money? I'll marry her," Asher said, "and you get her money. We'll both be happy."

Marry her? Marry her? Isabelle's eyes widened, and she tried to raise herself from the horse. Joel pushed her down.

Surely she'd misheard. What about his bad blood? His desire to end his family line? Why would he say such a thing? Was he...genuine? Did that mean he felt some affection for her as well?

Isabelle's cheeks warmed, and not just from the position where the blood was rushing to her head. The wild beating of her heart was from something completely different now. She refused to let herself think that his offer was only one of kindness. He was a man of his word. If he'd offered marriage, he was sure to follow through. But how did she feel about that? And would Joel even agree?

"Not good enough," Joel said. "I'm not interested. What I want, you can't give me."

"And what's that?" Asher asked.

Isabelle felt the gun press harder into her. She held as still as she could. Joel hissed, and she knew his words were likely going to be the last she ever heard. Closing her eyes, she prayed. *Dear God, please protect Asher. Help him to realize that he's not responsible for the things his family did, and that he's a good person, who can make a change for his family tree because I don't think I'll be around to tell him that again.*

"I want her to suffer," Joel said.

This is it. He's going to kill me.

"The same way I did, every time I looked at her."

"Asher...please. Get to safety," she begged, even though she knew he couldn't hear her. She couldn't bear the idea of him, someone who cared so much about others, being hurt because of her.

"You've a lot of darkness in your heart, if you want your own blood to suffer," Asher said. He sounded close. So close. Isabelle looked up as best as she could, but couldn't see him from her angle.

"Then I guess we don't have a deal," Joel laughed.

There was the cocking sound of a gun and then a shot, right next to her.

Isabelle screamed. The sound tore from her lips and she frantically tried to see what had happened. Had she been shot? Had Asher? She struggled, and soon realized the horse was at a walk, then a step. She slid off the horse, hurrying away from Joel, feeling the blood rush from her face. Lightheaded, she tried to run. Her legs fought her, wobbling and tripping her.

She was next. Where to go? There was no place to run. Nowhere to hide. The man who had been with Joel kicked his horse and rode, but two other men were closing in on him.

Isabelle turned then, ready to meet her destiny head on, whether it was that of her life or her death. Tears clouded her eyes but, chin up, she refused to let them fall. Her lips trembled, and her breath caught as her eyes took in the scene before her.

Asher stood about two feet from her. He had a hand outstretched, and without thinking, she ran to him, safe in his embrace. He crushed her to him as she asked, "What happened?"

"I shot first," was all he said. Then he pulled back. "Let me help you get your hands free."

As the blood worked its way back into her fingers, Isabelle massaged her hands. They stung, and she'd likely have bruises around her wrists, but she didn't care.

"You found me," she said, smiling up at him with relief.

"It was good timing when that wagon cover blew off," he told her then. "Not only could I be sure it was you, it startled them so much, they slowed."

"I'm so glad it worked," Isabelle said.

"Worked? That was your doing?"

She nodded proudly. "Yes."

He wrapped an arm around her, then moved to examine her. "Are you hurt?"

Isabelle shook her head. "No, I'm fine. Is Joel..."

"He's injured, but not dead." Asher nodded toward the second man who was now also captured. "They'll both be brought before a judge. You'll be safe. Attempted murder after all, but that's not all he's done. Not if what my deputy suspects is right."

"What's that?" Isabelle asked curiously as she saw Joel dragged to his feet and secured with ropes tightly.

"Several bank thefts," Asher told her. "That's enough to get a man hung, but it's not my job to say or to dole out the punishment." His eyes grew cold. "Lucky for him it's not."

Isabelle tucked her hand into the crook of his arm. "Thank you for coming after me. I wasn't sure anyone would find me. Or would even look for me."

He looked down at her, and his eyes roamed over her face. "I told you I'd protect you."

She swallowed hard. She had to do it. Had to let him out of the offer he'd made to Joel. "I know," she said, forcing a smile onto her lips. "You told me you look after the people in your town."

"That's not all," Asher said. "You. I look after you. I want to look after you."

Isabelle stilled. In just a matter of hours, everything had changed. She'd gone from being a woman on the run, to one captured, kidnapped, and rescued. Joel would be locked away or dealt with some other way, and she'd be free to do whatever. The problem was, what did she want to do?

Joel locked eyes with her as he was tied onto a wagon. He spit on the ground, then said, "This isn't over yet."

"I think it is," Asher answered.

Isabelle walked closer. She was no longer afraid of Joel. She'd realized that good did triumph. Quietly, she said, "Joel, you're right." She saw everyone's head snap to her, and continued, "Justice will be served, and like you said to me earlier today, soon you'll be enjoying everything you deserve."

There were chuckles as Joel was led away. The deputy approached, one hand resting on his belt. "The wagon should be good enough to take back slowly. Got the horses hitched to it again. Why don't you two use it?" he suggested to Asher.

"Ah—the front seat this time, please," Isabelle said with a small laugh. All of the men laughed, and Asher helped her into the seat, then climbed next to her. He took the reins, and set out, following behind the others slowly.

They rode in silence for a while. Spring Falls finally rose on the horizon, and at the sight of it, Isabelle sighed.

"You okay?" Asher asked, his face filled with concern.

"Yes, I just can't believe it might be over. That I can stop running. Looking over my shoulder." She opened her mouth to say more, to mention his offer of marriage, even though it hadn't been genuine, then closed her mouth again.

"You've more on your mind," Asher said. "What is it? Joel? His accomplice? I won't let either of them get near you again."

She smiled then. "That might be a little hard," she said lightly. "You might not always be around."

"Why not?" he asked.

Isabelle answered, "Because I don't live in this town. Eventually, I must decide to either continue on with my original plan, or return home, if I am needed to take care of things because of Joel's...absence."

She watched as her words sank in. Asher worked his jaw, then said, "You could stay."

"No one's asked me to," she answered. "Proper like." She glanced at him. "I can hardly consider your willingness to take my hand in marriage when you were shouting to Joel as we raced on horses to be genuine. I know it was just an attempt to save my life."

He was quiet. The wagon pulled in front of the sheriff's office, where a flurry of activity was happening.

"You should go," Isabelle said. "You are needed here."

"I need to make sure you are safe," Asher replied stubbornly.

Isabelle took a deep breath. "Wanting to make sure someone is safe is very different from wanting to looking after someone because you love them." She leaned close, brushed her lips against his cheek, and then climbed out of the wagon.

Isabelle didn't look back as she headed to the boarding house. She couldn't. It was obvious there was no reason for her to stay.

Chapter 23

"What will you do now?" Mrs. Donovan asked, twisting her apron in her hand. "I feel responsible, and I am so sorry."

"Nothing is your fault," Isabelle assured the woman. "With Joel gone, eventually I will be needed for any issues pertaining to my father's estate, and then maybe I'll find a good place to settle down. In fact, I've been hearing about a place, only about a half day drive that sounds quite nice."

"You're leaving? Where are you going to go?" Asher asked, leaning against the doorframe.

Isabelle hadn't heard his footsteps, and froze.

"I'll just leave you two alone," Mrs. Donovan said, and took a few steps back. "But not too alone. Door open, Sheriff. Man of the law or not, rules are rules, especially in my house."

Taking a deep breath, Isabelle didn't glance over as she continued to pack, instead listening to Mrs. Donovan's footsteps fading away. "There's a town nearby called Cottonwood Falls. I thought I might go see what's there."

"Cottonwood Falls? I've been there. In fact, a few years back, I was called to help with a search when a woman and the doctor went missing. Her name was Caroline. Matter of fact, she had someone chasing after her too." He stopped, and toed the ground. "She married the man who saved her."

Isabelle's heart did a tiny jump. "Oh?"

"Hear they're pretty happy," he continued. "Maybe like we could be."

She stilled. "I thought you weren't going to get married? Ever. You were going to end your family bloodline, or so you told me, several times." Isabelle turned then, knowing her tone was sharp, her expression one of challenge. "So, what does it matter to you where I go or what I do?"

Hurt flashed across his face, and she apologized. "I'm sorry. That was unkind of me. I appreciate your help in keeping me safe and rescuing me. I can see just how devoted you are to each of the people in your town."

"Not just the people in the town," Asher said. "I mean, I'd have gone after any of them. But you..." he stopped, and swallowed hard.

Isabelle tried not to show she was having trouble breathing. That her chest was tight with anticipation. "I what?" she finally asked, when the pause had lasted too long.

"You are different." Asher shrugged then, and his eyes met hers. "You're right. I didn't want to get married. The idea of passing along the traits in my family scare me to death. But when you were taken, one thing scared me even more."

"What's that?" Isabelle whispered.

"Being without you," he said, and stepped into her room. He glanced down then, realized what he'd done and stepped back.

With a small smile, Isabelle stepped forward, meeting him in the doorway. Asher reached out and took her hands in his. She was surprised at how nice that felt. How comfortable.

"The thought came to me that if I couldn't get you back or if something happened to you, my life would never be the same. When I saw him, that gun pressed into you, knowing that in the blink of an eye you could be gone, that, that right there, is when I knew what I'd been trying to not think about since I first met you."

"And what's that?" Isabelle asked.

"That I care about you," Asher told her. "That I don't want you to leave. I want you to stay here and for us to have a chance to see if we could make something happen between us."

Isabelle was quiet for a moment. Then she nodded. "I could do that," she agreed, and then raised her chin and grinned at him. "I might even like the idea of that."

"Do you?" Asher said. He stepped forward and pulled her into his arms.

Isabelle closed her eyes and leaned in for the kiss she was sure he was going to give her, when a loud, "Ahem," startled her.

"Outside the room," Mrs. Donovan said, shaking a kitchen towel at them.

Isabelle glanced down and saw Asher's boots a half step into her room. They backed up, and once Mrs. Donovan had nodded in satisfaction and continued on her way, Asher leaned down and gave her a kiss then pulled back.

"I'm glad you are giving me this chance, Isabelle," he said. "I am going to spend every moment trying to prove to you how much I love you. I hope you'll say yes when I ask you to marry me."

Isabelle smiled up at him and whispered, "Oh, I will. I'm very excited about it. There's also a lot to plan, so let's not wait too long."

He sucked in his breath then, his eyes wide. "Does that mean..."

She waited a moment, and when he didn't answer, teasingly poked his chest. "Does that mean what, Sheriff? You never finish your sentences."

"Does that mean you'll marry me?" he asked.

Isabelle turned away so he couldn't see the smile on her lips and the giggle that wanted to come out, and crossed her arms. "You've not asked me yet. Aren't you supposed to ask someone something if you want an answer?"

"Then let me fix that," Asher said, and stepped in front of her. "Miss Bowman, would you do me the honor of becoming my wife?"

Isabelle wrapped her arms around him. "Oh yes, Asher. Yes, I will."

Epilogue

Asher stood in front of his office, one hand gripping his mug.

"I smell trouble," Jeff said. "Sense it as thick in the air as the dust. Speaking of, when you think we're going to get rain?"

"Don't know," Asher said. "But I do know part of the trouble, and I think we'll be all right this time."

Jeff raised one eyebrow. "That so?"

"I asked Isabelle to stay a few days ago. To marry me," he said.

Jeff let out a low whistle. "That's trouble alright," he agreed. "I hope she can tolerate you."

"That's what Mrs. Donovan said," Asher agreed.

"I think she'll do just fine," Jeff said, and slapped his friend's shoulder. "I knew the right one would come along. Just didn't expect her to be on the stage, with another man chasing after her to take her life."

"Neither did I," Asher admitted. "Truth be told, I didn't think I'd ever get married."

"Things work out as they will," Jeff said mildly. Then he asked, "What news about her brother?"

"Tried and sentenced," Asher said. "All his property forfeit, since it appeared there was additional evidence found he'd been extorting their father. Judge decided he'd already had his inheritance, and now justice is going to be served. Isabelle will inherit everything."

"She know that?" Jeff asked.

"She does. Both about her brother and the inheritance." He was quiet a moment. "She told me that as difficult as it was to hear, the brother she'd known had died years before, and she'd already mourned his loss."

"Sounds like quite a woman," Jeff said. "Both of you come by for dinner Sunday. Becky wants to meet her."

Asher nodded, then straightened and set his mug down. "Here's the rest of the trouble," he said, as the blacksmith chased a group of boys down the street.

Setting his mug down as well, Jeff said, "I'll get the one in the blue shirt this time. Been a while since I chased after him. He's slippery. I need the exercise after that fritter."

"...and if I catch you in my forge again, I'll put you to work!" the smith yelled, puffing as he tried to catch the boys.

"No need to delay that," Asher called, easily grabbing two of the boys. "Today's as fine as any. Let's go, boys," he said, marching them in the direction of the smith.

"Actions have consequences," Jeff was saying to the boy in the blue shirt, as he hauled him up the street. "Both good and bad."

They sure do, Asher thought to himself, as he caught a glimpse of Isabelle on the sidewalk. She smiled and waved at him, and he nodded back.

Sometimes, those consequences turn out to be pretty darn good.

Note from Author

Thank you for taking the time to read Asher's Secret
Could I ask for one small favor? Reviews like yours on
Amazon mean so much to me and help others to find my
books! Even just a single line means a lot!

Want a FREE book?
Stop by my website to get your no strings attached **FREE
book**. It's my gift to you, as a thank you for reading this
book.
www.sarahlambbooks.com

Keep reading

Want to learn more about Cottonwood Falls?

Read Caroline's Story, then make sure you visit my website to get her free novella, Caroline's Gift.

Caroline Watson has been living at Mrs. Hardy's School for Girls since she was orphaned. When forced into marriage by the headmistress, she plots a desperate escape the night before to the furthest place her money will take her.

Even as he tells himself he is uninterested in the beautiful brunette who appeared off the stagecoach like an angel, Dr. Edward Mason finds himself attracted to Caroline. Still, he's determined that no one is going to tempt him into a relationship ever again.

Pushed together, Edward offers Caroline a job. Just as she's comfortable and settled in, a strange man comes to town and follows her. Now she's faced with a choice. Ask for help or run again.

Find Caroline here on Amazon:

https://www.amazon.com/Caroline-Runaway-Brides-West-Book-ebook/dp/B0B2N32YP5

About the Author

Sarah is wife to an amazing teacher and mom to two boys who are growing up just a little too fast. Her day job is helping others to become writers, while she squeezes in each spare moment she can on her own books. She spends her days working and writing in the Blue Ridge Mountains and planning her next trip to Disney World.

There are other great books in this series as well!

Find all the Winning His Devotion books on Amazon.

https://www.amazon.com/dp/B0CKBQTVGD

Want more of Sarah's books?

Find them all on Amazon!

https://www.amazon.com/stores/Sarah-Lamb/author/B098H3SGLK